PETER KOZMAR

Double Cross

DOUBLE CROSS

CHAPTER 1

Andy shivered from the cold and pulled the zipper of his jacket up higher as the chill from the damp river air seeped through his clothing. He twisted the rubber grip on the outboard motor making the rigid inflatable boat accelerate rapidly towards his goal. The white water the boat left in its wake worried him as it made him easy to spot in the darkness. For ten nervous minutes Andy sped up river until the bright lights of the warehouse gave an eerie glow in the distance. A short time later the illuminated structure came fully into his view and Andy eased the outboard motor down; the roar of the boat's engine fell to a gentle rumble and slowed the inflatable down to a crawl. Andy looked behind, to his relief the wake had all but gone. *Okay so far,* he told himself.

The bright lights of the warehouse combined with the height of the wharf, created a long shadow over the water which he exploited as he maneuvered the inflatable boat alongside the wharf's ladder, precisely where he'd been told it would be. Andy cut the engine, slowing the inflatable further as it pushed against the river's current then bumped against the ladder bringing the inflatable to a gentle stop. His heart quickened as he rushed forward and used a black nylon rope to secure the boat against the ladder. With the boat secure, he gripped the ladder with both gloved hands; the constant exposure to the river made its aging metal slippery and tricky to get a firm grip. Tentatively, he pushed down on the first rung with his right boot, it took his weight, and he slowly started to climb.

Reaching the top, he peered over the edge of the wharf and could see one of the external lights from the warehouse was broken. His confidence grew further – his asset had been right – the broken light formed a dark area around the only access door along this side of the long structure. With his head above the side of the wharf, Andy carefully looked around and listened for signs of the guards he knew would be patrolling the area. He slowed his breathing and hoped his heart rate would drop from racing to just pounding in his chest.

All looks clear, he told himself. His asset had said that – tonight – the side door would be unlocked. He wrapped his right arm around the ladder and checked his watch … one–twelve am. He remained in position as he watched the seconds tic away on his watch … one–fourteen … *move!*

Andy climbed the last five rungs quickly, stepped onto the wharf and, without pausing, ran towards the relative safety of the dark shadow covering the access door. With his back to the structure, he checked his watch again … *the guards will be changing shifts about … now.* He had less than five minutes to get in, find what he was looking for, gather evidence and get out. It was not with-out risk; there remained a possibility he could be discovered by a security guard running late for the shift change.

Andy reached for the door handle, pulled it down and gave it a gentle push with his shoulder … the door cracked open an inch. He peered inside the warehouse … it was still clear. *Now or never!* Andy drew his silenced pistol from his shoulder holster and pushed the door open wide enough for him to slip inside, quickly closing the door behind him (nothing signaled the presence of an intruder more than an unexpected open door). He immedi-ately crouched down and scanned the cavernous space lit by a dull yellow hew cast from the old roof lights.

The warehouse seemed eerily quiet. There were no signs of movement, unusual noises or the hushed voices of guards talking. *This is a bit odd, stay focused!* he told himself. Looking round he could see a number of wooden crates in long rows stacked three high. Andy stood slowly and, with his pistol raised, moved towards the nearest crate, his rubber-soled boots muffling the sound of his footsteps.

As he reached the first stack he put the pistol into his holster and, using both hands, opened the lid of the top crate; inside were freshly minted assault rifles. Carefully closing the lid he moved to the next stack of crates; this time, grenades ... Russian F1's. His asset had been right: the arms shipment had arrived. Then, set slightly away from the others, a single crate ... *there you are!*

Andy approached the single crate and removed his small black backpack. He opened it and removed a palm-sized digital camera, white cotton gloves, long thick black rubber gloves and a military grade respirator. He made sure the three atropine injectors were easy to reach by placing them on the floor by the crate ... even with the respirator and gloves he was still at risk of nerve agent poisoning; the injectors were a '*fail safe*' and may just save his life if exposed.

He slipped his hands into the cotton gloves before pulling on the thick black rubber pair up to his elbows. He donned the respirator and pulled the straps which tighten the seal of the mask against his face. His peripheral vision was restricted, but he'd rather have that constraint than die an agonizing death within minutes of opening the crate.

His asset said the chemical shells and the arms shipment were headed for Saddam Hussein's murderous regime in Iraq. Andy's orders from Langley were simple: gather evidence and leave without being detected. His heart raced at the thought of getting this close to lethal chemical munitions; one tiny drop would kill him. Andy felt nauseous and could feel the sweat forming on his forehead and inside the respirator making the eyepieces fog up.

He closed his eyes, took three deep breaths, then, after a final look around (to check he was still alone), he lifted the lid and looked inside the crate. *What the … heck!* Andy was stunned at what he saw.

The yellow radioactive hazard symbol wasn't what he expected. Andy looked down at the objects and quickly realized they were nuclear tipped battlefield artillery shells. Desperate for more clues he reached inside for the packing slip. The Russian writing on the paperwork identified the consignment as 152mm 3BV3 nuclear shells and, according to the slip, they were heading for Iraq. Andy's hands had a slight tremble as he took photos of the warheads and shipment paperwork. He replaced the paperwork, closed the lid and photographed the external marking on the crate.

Andy had a dilemma. Should he complete his mission and leave or stop nuclear weapons falling into the hands of Saddam Hussein? His mission had been based on information about chemical weapons. *Would my mission have been the same if Langley knew they were moving nuclear warheads?* he asked himself.

He removed the respirator and sucked in several deep breaths of damp air, then returned the respirator and camera to his backpack. Andy hesitated before removing the gloves but wearing them made it impossible for him to use his pistol so he didn't have much of a choice; death would be quick if he couldn't use his pistol and he wasn't ready to die … not today anyway! Andy took both pairs off and placed them all in his pack which he closed and secured. He checked his watch … one–nineteen. *I need to get out of here, I've got what I came for … no need for heroics*, he told himself, *but what about the warheads*?

He looked around and saw a pallet trolley by the wall of the warehouse. Andy cautiously made his way over to the trolley (constantly checking if anyone was around), brought it back and fed its two forks easily in the gaps underneath the pallet so he could raise it and pull it to the door … *Result!* … he felt very pleased with himself … and that was when he heard the voices, two of them, and they were getting louder … *Shit!*

Andy abandoned the trolley and quickly moved to a darker area, squeezing between two tall pallets he became nearly invisible in between the lines of crates. He removed his pistol from its holster and held it steadily with his right hand, keeping it pointed at chest height. He felt a single bead of sweat slowly work its way down his forehead, right cheek then down onto his neck; his dry mouth added to his discomfort. Steadying his breath, he worked out there were two guards and listened to their conversation as they neared his hiding place.

"Tomorrow all of this will be gone."

"This is the third shipment this month. Why would the torch bearers send all of this to Iraq?"

Andy wasn't sure that he had caught what was being said … *Did he say lantern bearer, torch carrier, lantern carrier?* There were a number of different meanings to what he'd heard. A lack of accuracy would be a failure on his part.

"It's always about the money."

The two men laughed as they walked away. Andy lowered his weapon, slowly squeezed out from his hiding space and looked around to check that the two guards had moved before committing himself to return to the trolley. Satisfied he was relatively safe, he tucked his pistol into its holster and headed to the door. To keep it open he applied a small wooden wedge which he found to the right of the door.

Andy struggled as he pulled the trolley outside. With thirty meters of open ground and a ladder to reach his boat, he felt both exposed and vulnerable. Andy removed the wedge and closed the door then looked around and listened for a few seconds. Nothing caught his attention, the only sounds he could hear were the gentle hum from the warehouse exterior lights and the low rumble of the moving water from the river. The coast looked clear.

Time to go, he whispered quietly to himself.

The weight of the munitions in the crate made moving the trolley over the open ground hard work. Even though the night air was just above freezing he could feel perspiration forming under his arms and beads of sweat on his forehead. Less than a minute later he was standing next to the ladder looking down at his inflatable boat four meters below.

His dilemma returned: leave the shells behind or find some way of taking them with him. He didn't want to leave the shells but his options were limited to ... none! *There's no way I can get the shells into the boat*, Andy admitted to himself. He knew he didn't have the strength and dexterity to carry the shells down to the boat one by one – the wharf ladder was way too slippery – and dropping them from this height would more than likely sink it. *I'll just have to ditch them and hope the water does the rest*, he decided.

Andy hauled the trolley a few meters further forward until he judged it was clear of his boat, then pushed the crate with all his strength so that it toppled into the deep water below. The loud splash, as it hit the water, was amplified by the stillness of the night. *Damn!* Andy looked down to see the crate sink as the dark water quickly consumed it ... *time to move* ... but he had paused for a second too long, as he stood up to climb onto the ladder and start his descent into the safety of the shadows, he heard someone shout loudly behind him.

"Hey, you!"

Whoever it was wasn't waiting for a reply; Andy heard the eruption of gunfire and then the crack of a bullet as it passed close overhead. *Good job they aren't a good shot!* Andy moved quickly onto the ladder and slid down it without using the rungs. As he reached the bottom he slowed his descent and neatly stepped off the last rung of the ladder into the boat. He knew he'd bought himself precious seconds and, under the cover of the wharf he was safe, but now '*they*' were closing in on his position above. *I need to get out of here … pronto*, he told himself.

Andy untied the boat, moved to the rear of the inflatable and pulled the rip-start on the engine – nothing happened – he opened the choke and pulled the rip-start again. The sixty-horsepower engine made no effort to start. *Shit! Not now!* He pulled the rip-start again … still nothing … *this isn't good* … his heart was racing. He could hear the shouts getting closer; if he didn't move quickly they would be right on top of him.

Andy tried to think back to his training at the Farm (they'd had a session on small boat handling), then he remembered what to do and quickly applied three firm squeezes to the fuel bulb. *Now would be good*, he thought as he pulled the rip-start again. The engine turned … it didn't fire but it had made an effort and that was progress! His arms were starting to ache, "Come on!" he shouted at the stubborn outboard engine … *I don't want to have to swim!*

He gave the rip-start one last chance and pulled hard; he really didn't want to have to swim. The engine fired and roared to life. *Yes!* Andy pulled the gear lever towards him and twisted the grip sending the inflatable forwards rapidly along the side of the wharf. *The longer I can use the wharf for cover the* better. When he reached the end of the wharf, where the river narrowed, Andy turned the inflatable in a large arc to get as close as possible to the far river bank.

The lights from the warehouse illuminated him as he drove the boat hard and fast down the river. The white wash from the boat's wake made him easier to spot, but all he cared about was getting away. The air lit up with lines of red tracer which zipped angrily around him and, then, the water started to dance as the rounds that followed missed their intended target ... him! It felt like minutes, but could only have been seconds, before he was finally out of the glare of the warehouse lights and into the darkness. He felt relief wash over him as he reached the bend in the river and safety from the gunfire.

CHAPTER 2

Andy glanced at his watch to check the time. He had two minutes before his appointment with Carrie Roper. He paused for a moment, looked down to make sure his shoes were clean and the zipper on his trousers was done up. *Ready*. He knocked on the door to Roper's office.

"Come!" came the command from inside. Andy opened the door and stepped inside. "Close the door behind you," she instructed as she pointed with her pen at the door through which Andy had just entered. With the door closed, Roper used her pen to point to the chair in front of her desk, "Sit". Andy did as he was told and sat. He looked at her desk, apart from the obligatory cozy family photography, the only other item on her desk was his mission report.

"Okay, Flint, I've read your report. Just remind me what were your mission parameters?" she asked.

"Undertake a covert entry into the warehouse facility and gather evidence of the supply of chemical munitions to the Government of Iraq."

"Were you instructed to move any of the munitions?" she probed.

"No." *This isn't going as I hoped, I wonder where she's going with this.*

"Did you remove any of the munitions and, in doing so, draw attention to yourself drawing gunfire from the security forces at the location?"

"I didn't remove any of the munitions, I merely … moved them."

Roper leaned forward: "Don't get clever with me, Flint, it would not be a good career move!" She leaned back and pointed to his report with her pen. "Did the instruction to move the weapons come from your mission briefing?"

Andy felt anger start to boil within him. "I was briefed on, and equipped to deal with, chemical weapons. What I found were nuclear warheads and I wasn't briefed on those so I improvised. Our intelligence was wrong; the job I was sent to do changed as soon as I opened that crate. Maybe you should be asking your sources how they managed to get it so wrong instead of questioning my judgement. As you've pointed out before, you aren't a field agent, so excuse me if I have to follow my instincts and deviate from the mission I was briefed on; until you are in that position you will have no idea what it's like to be so wrong footed." Andy lost his cool and immediately regretted doing so, but he'd made his point!

Roper recoiled by the unexpected change of tack and countered: "The success of this operation is open to question: on one hand, you stopped nuclear weapons falling into the hands of a pariah state; on the other, you alerted the bad guys that we're on to them. In doing that, you may have compromised a valuable source," she held her right hand up to stop Andy from replying, "Langley are working through your report and will decide on what happens to you."

"Is there something going on which I should be aware of?" Andy enquired wondering why there appeared to be so much angst over a mission that, as far as he was concerned, had gone better than expected: he'd gathered evidence on the warheads, placed them temporarily out of reach and returned safely. Roper looked away for a brief moment then picked up his report.

"The way you handled the defection of Colonel Shanina, you

went outside the agency and teamed up with the FBI," Roper shook her head as she continued, "you didn't make any friends ... quite the opposite actually." Her words hung in the air between them.

That was months ago ... and I was fully debriefed at the time. Why bring this up now, where's she going with this. Cagily he responded, "Shanina's defection helped shut down a number of Russian operations and helped us turn some of those, traitors, into double agents for us."

"Flint, you worked with the FBI and cut our chain of command out of the loop, you chose to work with the other team ... some at Langley don't see you as a team player ... they don't trust you."

"Do you trust me?" he asked. Roper broke eye contact and looked at the pen in her left hand. *I'll take that as a 'no' then!*

"While Langley are reviewing this," she tossed the file onto her desk, "I'm placing you on leave ... indefinitely. You would do well to use this time to decide if you're suited to the job or whether your '*talents*' are more useful elsewhere; either way it's out of my hands ... close the door on your way out."

***

Andy arrived at the Moscow Chamber Opera Theatre off Nikolskaya Street a few minutes before four. Since there were no performances that week he knew Lenya wouldn't need to work late. In the weeks since his return from the US, Andy had slowly got to know Lenya. They'd gone on a few dates and he was keen to see more of her. He hoped she felt the same way about him, but while he'd been trained to read people, with her he couldn't be sure. When he wore his heart on his sleeve and viewed his date through rose colored spectacles, his ability to read people tended to be out of focus and his blind-spot gave way to insecurities which nagged away at the back of his mind.

He went through the main doors, headed past the unattended

box office counter and through the side door towards the administration offices at the back of the theater. It struck Andy, as he headed for Lenya's office, that unlike the front of house, the back office area needed new carpets, a fresh lick of paint and better lighting. This whole place was run down. But then again, it wasn't part of the show and, back in its heyday, would never have been seen by senior Communist Party officials. He stopped by the bright blue door for Lenya's office, a dull brass sign read '*Administratsiya*'. He knocked on the partially open door and walked straight in.

Lenya's face lit up the moment she saw him but she couldn't speak as she was on a phone call; instead she waved. Andy listened to her and from what he heard he gathered she was talking about catering arrangements for a private function ... something about a string quartet performing during the lunch break for an investment bank's strategy session booked into one of the theater's function rooms. Lenya hung up, stood and rushed over to Andy, firmly embracing him and planting a kiss square on his lips. "You have surprised me ... thank you," she said smiling.

"I finished work early. So I thought what better way to spend my time, but with you," he replied sheepishly. Like most of the Russians he had contact with, Lenya was in the dark about what he did and who he worked for ... unlike Vladim, he wasn't ready to trust her with that information ... yet! She kissed him again. "How about dinner and then to a jazz night. I heard one of our sister charities is sponsoring a US jazz group," he suggested.

Lenya looked puzzled. "Why would a charity sponsor a jazz tour?" she asked.

"It's a long story. But the short version is the jazz group is made up of members from deprived inner city areas. The tour helps show those communities that there are ways out of the ghettos other than via the justice system." She still looked puzzled as he continued, "It means they have choices and opportunities in life which don't all lead to prison".

Lenya smiled again: "Sounds like a great idea!" she released Andy, reached for her coat and handbag, "I'm ready … let's go!" Stepping out onto the sidewalk Lenya linked arms with Andy and pulled him close.

***

Andy woke late the following day and just before lunch headed over to Vladim's new offices. Vladim smiled when Andy walked through the door. "What are you doing here? Have you been fired?" Vladim joked, but seeing the pained look on Andy's face made him realize he'd hit a sore spot so he waited for Andy to reply.

"I thought we'd go for lunch and maybe have a few beers." Andy offered.
"Just wait a few minutes. I have a few things I need to finish off then we can have a leisurely lunch and catch-up."

"I'll wait out there." Andy asked pointing at the door.

Vladim nodded his agreement and returned to his paperwork. Andy headed into the main office and looked at Vladim's writing on the large white boards which hung on the walls. The writing had details of customers who needed urgent computer deliveries together with quantities, part numbers and expected delivery date. Four staff busied themselves behind their computer screens. They looked happy and the office had a good vibe about it as two more staff arrived carrying take-out food. The atmosphere felt very different to the previous office where Popov and his men were their most regular visitors and intimidation was the order of the day.

Andy made his way towards the back rooms and peered into the large kitchen where, to one side, he saw a pool table with the balls arranged and stacked to play. To the right of the pool table a two-seater couch had been positioned in front of a television, two Play Station controllers rested on the floor in front of the couch; their leads snaked to the console which was hooked up to the bulky television.

On the other side of the kitchen was a large fridge, a cheap plastic table with four white plastic chairs and a battered microwave oven pushed against the wall. Further to the left was a small table with an electric kettle next to the tea and coffee. The two staff with the take-out food headed over to the sink and opened the top right-hand drawer to remove cutlery, before moving past Andy to the table and chairs. *Functional*, he thought to himself.

He approached the sink and reached up to an open cupboard for a cup. As his hand touched the jar of instant coffee he was disturbed. "Come on, let's go." Vladim called out from the doorway. He was already wearing his jacket and ready to head out. A few minutes later they were taking their seats at a local restaurant which had yet to fill with lunchtime patrons. What started as a quiet meal with a glass of vodka soon turned into an afternoon with two bottles of vodka and a few glasses of Bourbon. The two men shared jokes and each tried hard to out brag the other with their various tales. Late in the afternoon Vladim looked at his watch and appeared sad.

"My friend, I'm going to have to call this a day. I still have work to do. We should catch up later in the week, maybe one evening."

"That sounds like a good idea," Andy agreed enthusiastically, his speech betraying a slight slur. He wasn't used to drinking as much alcohol as he'd just consumed with Vladim, who still appeared sober. On the way out the two men settled the bill and said their '*goodbyes*' with their usual warm hug. Andy decided to clear his head and walk back to the safe house where he was staying. The alcohol had dulled his senses enough for him not to notice the two women following him at a discreet distance.

When Andy arrived at the safe house he found he'd received a blunt email from Carrie Roper: "Your leave is over. Return to work with immediate effect." *Great! They must have decided I did the right thing.*

***

Entering the Embassy, Andy felt refreshed and relaxed. He dropped his bag when he got to his desk and fired up his computer then, as it gradually whirled into action, he went to the kitchen and grabbed a black coffee. He took one sip and almost spat it out … *jeez this is as bad as ever!* Returning to find his computer ready for action … he checked his emails.

He had one message … tagged as *'Urgent'.* It originated from Roper. Andy clicked on the email. He read the brief message*:* 'Come *to my office as soon as you read this.' Okay?* Andy didn't get any *'feel good vibes'* from her words. He locked his computer and, with his coffee in hand, he headed to Roper's office. The door was open but he still knocked with his free hand and waited.

"Come!" Andy entered Roper's office. She had a large cup of coffee on her desk and a half eaten sweet pastry which he took to be her breakfast. "Close the door," she instructed wafting her pen in the general direction of the door. Andy closed the door. "Sit." He did as he was told.

"How was your time off?" she asked. *This isn't going to be good.* He felt uneasy.

"Um … Good. Very relaxing. Thanks."

"Some of the team said they saw you down at the gym," she said as she failed to create some sort of rapport between the two of them.

"Yes, it's a great gym. It's a good way to let off steam."

"Good," her expression changed, "Langley have come back with their review of your report."

"And?" he asked, offering her a nervous smile. Roper looked uncomfortable as she shifted position in her chair. Andy was immediately on his guard.

"In their opinion the nukes should have remained in place and undisturbed. Instead you made your presence known and prevented the weapons moving through the supply chain to Iraq, which we would have tracked. After you dumped them in the river, the Russian military turned up and recovered them."

She slowly placed a series of large black and white photographs face up on the table in front of Andy. Andy could tell she was enjoying the moment despite her straight face and monotone voice ... she wasn't professional, just very clinical at cutting through his outer layers and exposing his inadequacies.

The photographs in the sequence showed a military river barge, crane and divers recovering the nuclear shells from the riverbed. Apart from the divers, all the soldiers were dressed in full protective gear. The last picture in the sequence showed the empty wharf and no barge. "Naturally, the Russians denied any knowledge of missing their warheads."

"At least Saddam Hussein hasn't got them," he stated.

She gave him a tired expression: "Not this week anyway, but I've got some good news for you." Andy sat up. *Maybe I've been too pessimistic.*

"You're going back into the field and we have got an assignment for you which should keep you out of mischief ... it's been decided that you'll be running agents into Russia." Andy was puzzled. *Into Russia ... she did say ... into Russia?*

"Where will I be operating from?" he asked as casually as he could muster.

"Langley have an urgent need for someone to run assets from our field station in Luhansk."
What? No. That's a real shit hole ... they must be pissed with me.

"Ukraine. Did you offer to transfer me?"

Roper shook her head. "Two things. Firstly, it wasn't my call, the Station Chief in Luhansk got caught up in in a street robbery which ended badly – he's dead – and they need someone to take on some of his workload ... Langley believe that someone else is you; Secondly, you're not being transferred, it's an assignment ... you'll be back in Moscow in no time."

Andy tried his best to smile and not look angry at hearing the news of his *'punishment'*.

"Your cover is you work for an NGO helping rural growth and development in Eastern Europe. You know the brief. You're there to slow the migration to the big cities and help keep rural communities viable. You'll run assets over the border into Russia from the station in Luhansk."

"I guess it gives me a reason to travel across the area and mix with various communities."

Roper nodded. "Luhansk Station reports into the agency desk based in the Embassy in Kiev, which means, you're temporarily off my books until they find a Ukrainian speaker to fill the role. However, language won't be a problem as that region is mainly populated by ethnic Russians, so you'll get along just fine speaking Russian."

"How long will I be away from Moscow?" he asked.

She sucked on her teeth, looked up and to the right. "Keep your nose clean and get some good results ... maybe, six months."
The tension between them increased as he digested the information. His heart sank. *Six months minimum ... that's a lifetime!*

"Come on!" he protested, "there's so much happening right here, right now! Yeltsin is barely in control of the country. His parliament has defied him. His deputy has gone public denouncing him. Every day there are street protests against him. The military are undecided and could throw their support one way or the other. The whole country may implode any day now. It's right on a knife edge. We've got a queue of senior people in the Russian government offering their souls to us so they have a way out. Why would Langley order me out of the country and miss all of this?"

"I've told you … it wasn't my call," Roper looked him square in the eye, "you know I need you here." Andy looked hopeful. *Maybe Roper will fight to keep me!* "You know the people upstairs weren't happy with your last operation. They want you out of the way … for the moment. The situation in Luhansk gives them the opportunity to get you away from Moscow … for now … do a good job and they'll bring you back."

This sucks … but I'm not getting out of this … maybe I could get a small win. He sat up and leaned forward: "I get it's an important role for me and I'll not let you, or the agency, down," he paused for a second, "Would it be possible to swing it for me to take my girlfriend down there when I've move in? Having a Russian girlfriend around for a week or two would definitely help establish my cover," he said confidently.

"Is she that Russian working out of the theater?" Roper asked.

"Yes."

Roper considered the question briefly. "I agree it will help with your cover, but I will have to run it past Langley. I think I can persuade them it would be beneficial to the success of their mission to allow her to be funded with tickets."

"When do I leave?"

"Tomorrow."

CHAPTER 3

Andy purchased a bottle of Georgian red wine from a bottle store on his way to Lenya's family apartment on the outskirts of the city towards the East. From Lenya's description, her family lived on the sixth floor of a sprawling gray concrete tenement block. Walking briskly through the city he noticed a large column of armored troop carriers heading slowly towards the city center. It was impossible to miss the tanks and armed soldiers positioned at the major intersections. There were more troops scattered in public areas relaxing in the early evening sunshine.

Yeltsin's standoff with his Parliament is turning serious ... I wonder which side these soldiers are on?

He kept his head down, avoided eye contact and kept walking. Twenty minutes later Andy arrived in Lenya's neighborhood where he read the signage which indicated only service or delivery vehicles were permitted near the buildings ... all other vehicles were prohibited. This explained why all the parking lots were on the outskirts of the campus making it a pleasant area to walk through.

He counted twelve towering accommodation units arranged in a four by three grid, each connected by wide ground level walkways where children cycled and played ball games. Reaching Lenya's apartment block, he stepped into the stairwell and headed for the lifts noting that they were *'out of service'*. The fading graffiti indicated they'd been out of commission for some time. Andy shrugged and headed up the concrete stairs, two at a time, holding the wine bottle firmly in his hand.

Andy paused when he reached her apartment. He hadn't told her he would visit this evening so he knew it would be a surprise. His immediate departure to Luhansk meant he risked not seeing her if he didn't make this special journey. He felt nervous at the thought of meeting her parents for the first time. His nervousness further intensified because of the number of security protocols he knew he'd broken.

He'd not yet received the results of the background check on Lenya and her family; they could be a family of informers or part of the security services ... he didn't know ... didn't care. He'd not told anyone where he was going, therefore breaking another protocol, if anything unexpected happened or the police picked him up, he'd be on his own. However, unlike when he met Max Popov and his cronies for the first time, Andy felt the reassuring pressure of his 9mm semi-automatic. He breathed deeply, counted to three then knocked loudly.

"Who's there?" a woman's voice called out. It didn't sound like Lenya.

"Andy Flint, Lenya's friend," he replied. Through the solid steel door, he could hear excited voices speaking quickly amongst themselves. The voices were not quite loud enough for him to hear what they were saying.

"Is it really you?" a familiar voice called out.

"Yes, Lenya, it's me." He heard someone unlock the door which swung open revealing Lenya. When she saw him her eyes widened with surprise and her smile spread.

"What are you doing here?" she asked, at the same time, beckoned him inside.

"I come bearing gifts ..." he held up the wine bottle as he walked through the door.

"My parents would like to meet you," she said as she closed the door behind him. An elderly, gray haired couple stood together in the entranceway behind Lenya. Andy presented the wine to the man he assumed to be her father.

The man's face lit up as he read the label. "I've not had such fine Georgian wine in years. I'm looking forward to drinking this tonight."

"This is Andy Flint, the American I told you about. He works for a charity in the city." With the formal introduction over, Lenya's mother took Andy's arm and guided him through their apartment to the living room where she gestured for him to sit on a double settee.

She surprised Andy when she sat next to him, leaving Lenya to sit on a low, three legged wooden stool. Lenya's father momentarily disappeared returning with a bottle of vodka and four crystal glasses which he placed on the table. He opened the vodka and filled the glasses to their brims.

"How did you meet Lenya?" her mother quizzed.

"I was organizing a tour of the theater for work and while at the theater I saw Lenya and just had to speak with her." Lenya blushed.

"You like her lots, no?" she continued. This time it was Andy's turn to blush, Lenya looked to be enjoying his discomfort.

"Yes, I like her lots," he replied. Her father handed out the glasses of vodka, starting with Andy. Once the four of them were holding their glasses of vodka. Lenya's father raised his glass.

"A toast. To new friends."

"To new friends!" they repeated, draining their glasses in one hit.

"How long have you lived in Moscow? Where are you from in America? Do you have brothers and sisters? Do you want many children?" Lenya's mother bombarded him with questions as Lenya squirmed in her chair.

"Mother! Leave him alone. We've only just started dating," Lenya implored. *This is getting intense. I need to dial this down a few notches.*

"I've come around to tell Lenya something," he announced. Lenya's mother clasped her hands together and held them tightly to her chest. Her father looked suspiciously at Andy, then smiled at Lenya. Lenya just looked plain confused as she had no idea why Andy had come around to their apartment or know what he had come to say. The three of them hung on for his next words.

Andy stood in case they would ask him to leave. "Something has come up with work at short notice and I have to leave tomorrow." The smiles faded, the joyous atmosphere in the apartment fell flat. He couldn't look at Lenya as he continued, he felt a lump form in his throat. "I've been asked to go to the Ukraine for a few months and work at our office in Luhansk."

Lenya burst into tears. Her mother dropped her hands to the table, her face still fixed with a smile. Her father just said "I'll be damned. That's a surprise." Lenya stood, rushed across and embraced Andy with a hug as she cried. *These people must be really upset by what I've just told them.*

Lenya wiped the tears from her eyes and then her cheeks with her sleeve. "This is wonderful news" she said as she released him.

I'm confused. How is this good news? "Really?" was all he could say.

"We're from Alchevs'k. It's about 30 kilometers West from Luhansk. We have many relatives still living there. It would be wonderful to see them again."

Her father recharged their glasses with vodka and handed them out. "Another toast. To Luhansk!"

"To Luhansk!" they all called out as one and knocked the spirit back. As the vodka went down, he could feel it warm his stomach. He put his down glass, looked at Lenya and reached out for her hand.

"My grandparents still live near Luhansk and I have many aunties and uncles I'd like to meet."

"Keep an eye on uncle Vanya!" Lenya's father announced as he winked at Andy, "He's a bit of a rogue with very light fingers. Check you still have your watch after you've shaken his hand and check your wallet when you walk away." The room filled with laughter as the atmosphere changed for the better.

"I'm going to have to leave as I've got to pack for an early flight. But I did want to see you before I left," He smiled. "Let me know when you can come down for a week or two and I'll arrange your flights and send you the tickets … my treat!" he smiled. Lenya leaned over and gently kissed him on the cheek. Andy turned and headed for the door followed closely by Lenya. Her parents stayed back in the lounge giving them some privacy while they said their goodbyes.

CHAPTER 4

"In here is bathroom," the landlady pointed into a small windowless yellow room with a toilet, sink and low level hand shower. Andy caught the unpleasant whiff of stale piss as she closed the door. She led Andy through the lounge, with its tired looking settee and armchairs, towards the two bedrooms at the rear of the apartment. They were painted dark green, Andy presumed this was to hide signs of the mold that lurked nearby judging by smell of damp lingering in the air. Each bedroom was furnished with a double bed, two bedside cabinets with drab old-fashioned lamps which Andy doubted they worked, and large chest-of-drawers, but no wardrobes.

He stepped into one bedroom and peered out of the window, through the tobacco-stained net curtains, across the industrial estate with its heavy industry and chimneys belching their dark acrid smoke high into the sky. Today, with little wind, the smoke didn't dissipate very much adding to the depressing gray tones of the city of Luhansk. Beyond the industrial area he could just make out fields and woodlands and the main highway running East towards Russia. Out of the window and immediately to the right he saw a metal lattice structure with ladders. The landlady saw him look: "Fire escape," she said matter-of-factly. It took Andy a few seconds to figure it out as his eyes followed the rusting structure down to the ground. *I'm not sure I'd risk it!* Andy headed back into the lounge where the landlady had placed the paperwork on the dining table.

"You have no pets?" she asked, "only you. No family?" *What? You think I'd bring a family to this shit hole.*

"No pets, only me, maybe, my girlfriend," he replied.

The landlady nodded approval, then using her index finger, she tapped the paperwork: "You sign … one-hundred-dollar bond and one month rent in advance."

The guys in the field office had recommended this as one of the best apartment blocks to live in with the '*benefit*' of being only a short walk from the office. But, compared to Washington, New York or Moscow, Luhansk was a tiny backwater city … everywhere was a short distance from the office. The landlady presented Andy with a cheap blue plastic ballpoint pen. "There is much interest. You like, yes or no?" Andy took the pen from her then signed and dated the paperwork.

He reached for his wallet and removed two hundred dollars in twenty dollar notes. He counted the notes out onto the table; as he did so the old lady licked her lips. With his counting over, she scooped up the notes and placed them in her large brown handbag before she wrote out a receipt which she presented to him. "Ten dollars for prepay electricity card," she said as she held up a card the size of a credit card in her right hand, "fill it up downstairs at office or at the supermarket on main street." Andy started to peeled a ten dollar note from his wallet, but before he could pull out the cash, she added, "Card need credit … another ten dollars, I give you card with credit now." Andy smiled with resignation as he switched the ten for a twenty and handed it over to his new landlady. She quickly produced a second card from her pocket and pressed it into his hand, then rummaged in her handbag before producing two sets of door keys and handed them to him.

Each set had three keys. She saw him examining them. "One is for entrance door downstairs. The second is for your apartment and third is for shed out the back where the trash cans are kept. Garbage day is Friday."

"Thanks." Andy said as he stepped out of his *'new'* apartment into the communal hallway. He could hear music drifting through a neighbor's door. After a moment he recognized a Whitney Houston song. *With my door closed, I don't think this volume of music will disturb me.*

"You pick one of best apartments for rent in all of Luhansk. It even has inside toilet, exclusive for your use!" she bragged.

Andy sighed and shrugged his shoulders: "I'm so fortunate," he replied ... she beamed with pride ... his sarcasm completely lost on her!

***

A tall thin man with short brown hair opened the solid metal blue door. Andy wasn't expecting a field agent to be wearing a blue sports tracksuit and sneakers. The man smiled. "Andy, welcome to Station Lima!" He thrust his hand out, "Morgan Winchester." Andy shook his hand firmly and returned the smile.

Winchester invited him into his new workplace located above a family restaurant and only a short distance from his apartment. Winchester closed the heavy door behind him and they walked down a short corridor to another closed security door. A small camera above the door filmed his approach as an unseen observer buzzed the electronic lock to enter through the second door.

He stepped into a large room where two other field agents were waiting. "This is Nikoli Yevenko," Winchester indicating towards a bald man wearing denim pants and a black tee-shirt who raised a hand. "Over there is Dan Kowalski" Winchester continued the introductions as a bearded man stood up and approached Andy to shake hands.

"Some asshole in Langley thought my Polish ancestry was good enough to qualify me for three years in Ukraine. What's your story?"

"I went beyond the scope of my mission, the higher-ups didn't appreciate me showing creativity in the field and so ... here I am. I could be out in six months with good behavior." The men burst out laughing; Andy recognized that this was one of those 'yeah, right!' moments and, for the first time since learning of his posting, he felt a doubt surface that he may be in Luhansk longer than six months!

Winchester ended the laughter first: "That's what they said to me ... two years ago. Sent me to Kiev and then here, Station Lima." The laughter started again. "You got your accommodation sorted out?" Winchester asked as he gestured for Andy to sit on one of the three large settee's surrounding three sides of a low square wooden coffee table. Yevenko was first to sit, followed by Andy, Kowalski and Winchester.

"I've just signed. It's in the block you guys recommended." The three agents stifled their laughter as if sharing a private joke, their eyes darting between each other, looking to see if someone was going to crack and give the game away that they'd directed him to one of the crappier rentals in the city.

Winchester gathered himself together: "Good, over there is your security system which we'll help you install later on today," he pointed to two large brown packing boxes stacked in one corner. "Just the usual, extra locks, camera's, storage device for the video feeds, and bug sweeper. Okay, for phone calls, anything unclassified, use your cell phone; if it's confidential use the secure landline in here." Winchester pointed to a gray desk phone which rested on a table next to a computer monitor. To Andy the phone looked just like the ones he'd seen around Langley. "Kowalski is our crypto custodian so you don't have to worry about the daily key updates," he informed Andy.

"Understood," Andy said nodding his agreement to physically demonstrate his understanding.

The mood lightened a bit as Yevenko piped in: "It's quite a big operation we run from here, and we were starting to be spread a little thin and in need of extra resourcing, which is where you come in."

"What happened to the Station Chief?" Andy asked, "I heard he'd been robbed and it went wrong."

The three agents looked between each other and then Winchester spoke for them. "Is that what they told you?" his voice raised as he asked for clarification.

"Why would I make that up?" Andy replied suddenly feeling defensive.

Kowalski held his hand up to silence Winchester. "Our Station Chief, Danny Lynch, had trained in a number of martial arts and could easily whip the ass of anyone twenty years his junior. He knew how to handle himself, better than anyone in this room. He took a beating, then someone put four rounds into him. Three to the chest and one to the head, classic Russian Mafia execution if you want my opinion. But here's the thing, if it was a robbery as you said '*gone wrong*', why leave his watch, wallet and car keys behind?" The room fell quiet.

Andy broke the silence: "What do you guys believe happened?"

"We think it's connected to the events happening in Moscow, with the stand-off between the President and Parliament, and a large Russian troop build-up just a few miles from here across the border in Russia." Winchester was very clear and his words made more sense to Andy than the '*robbery gone wrong*' he'd been spoon-fed by Carrie Roper.

"The Russian Ministry of Defense has not declared any exercises or troop movements scheduled for that area," Yevenko added.

"Then we started losing assets. They'd go over the border and all would be fine. Suddenly they'd go silent and a few days later their bodies would be found," Winchester chipped in.

"Langley aren't paying attention. Their focus is elsewhere and don't want to believe what we're telling them. They've directed us to keep the local protocols unchanged. For example, we're to remain unarmed, that's unwise in my book," Yevenko continued, "but we'll provide you with weapons to store in your apartment for your personal protection. Should the threat assessment change … you may not have time to get over here and be issued with a weapon."

"What do the Russian's gain by murdering Lynch?" Andy asked.

"To reduced our capability at a time when they are murdering our assets and massing troops across the border … why else?" Kowalski replied.

"Well the sooner I'm up and running, the quicker I can help take on some of the workload. Are you guys ready to give a hand?" Andy pointed towards the two packing boxes. "As well as that security equipment, my gear has already arrived from Moscow."

The four men spent the afternoon moving Andy's gear into the rental, assembling his gun safe and installing the security system with its cameras and electronic locks. With the safe and the security system finally in place, Yevenko and Kowalski headed back to the office only to return twenty minutes later carrying two heavy looking black canvass holdalls.

"It's Christmas time!" Kowalski announced, as they walked in and threw the holdall he'd been carrying onto the kitchen table, it made a heavy metallic clatter when it landed. Yevenko, walked in behind and closed the front door carefully placing his holdall onto the same table.
Kowalski unzipped his bag and reached in to pull out an AR15 with an extended magazine attached. "Already loaded and ready to use." He produced two more full magazines placing them on the table, along with a 12-gauge pump-action shotgun and two

boxes of shells. Finally, he removed a 9mm Glock and four full magazines: "Remember to keep these locked in your safe."

Yevenko opened his holdall. One after another he produced four flash bangs. Then two tear gas grenades. "Now, what I'm about to give you isn't on our agency inventory, so don't go mentioning you have any of the following items or you'll end up in trouble and we'll deny knowing about it. Understood?" Andy eagerly nodded his understanding … it did feel like Christmas. Yevenko produced two M67 grenades. "These are live. They ain't training aides." He reached inside and produced two Claymore mines. "String these babies up. One out front. The other out back. I'm assuming you know how to fire these?" Andy nodded. He'd undertaken explosives training and handled different munitions at The Farm, but never used a Claymore. "You want some help setting these up?" Yevenko asked. Andy nodded again. He didn't want to accidentally set one off when putting it into position. "Okay. Let's do to it."

Five minutes later the Claymore mines were set. Andy looked at the two firing switches positioned on the table next to the large expensive TV which they'd somehow managed to maneuver into the apartment. It had been rigged to show the live camera feeds. To fire the Claymores, Andy only had to flick the switches safety cover up and throw the delicate metal switch. The switch on the left, would detonate the Claymore in the communal hallway, while the one on the right, would detonate the Claymore covering the fire escape. Andy knew that if he triggered a Claymore, its blast would kill anyone within fifty meters with its seven hundred steel balls of death. When they'd finished he felt safer and now they could head off to have a few well-earned beers.

***

After leaving Yevenko and Kowalski at the bar, he'd popped into a nearby store for groceries and cleaning equipment. Even with his fresh bedding he'd had a restless night sleep as the mattress was way too soft. That and his mind which raced over his fears about his posting to this forgotten backwater being longer than he'd been told. He'd finally drifted into a deep sleep just as his alarm clock went off.

Andy stifled a yawn when he entered the station and saw Winchester sat at the large, shared desk reading the overnight reports from Langley and Kiev.

"Good morning Morgan," Andy called out trying to sound up-beat and wide awake. Thankfully he could smell the welcoming aroma of fresh coffee waiting for him to grab a cup. He hoped it was strong cos he needed it to be if he was to stay awake.

"Morning Andy. You get yourself sorted out?" Winchester looked up from his screen.
"Yes I did, though it's not quite the same as my apartment in Moscow but I'll get used to it." Andy headed over to the kitchen unit and picked up a cup before finally reaching the coffee. "Any-thing interesting in the reports?"

"Not really. The instability in Russia has the Ukrainian Govern-ment on edge and looking to mobilize its own military forces. The debate will take a few weeks before they come to a con-clusion. There's an increase in Russian military radio traffic just across the border and, of course, the Russian Government is denying any military activity over and above what is normal this close to the border."

"What do you think is happening?"

"I know the Russians have increased their intelligence activities in and around Luhansk. They're pretty easy to spot when you know what to look for. Even the local press is reporting the Rus-sian military build-up just across the border. Our assets have confirmed it and we estimate there to be two Divisions of ar-mored infantry in position."

"What do you think they'll do?" Andy asked as he took a sip of the strong black coffee. It was nectar to his body and just the right punch to help him to wake up and focused. Winchester scratched his head, then answered.

"My gut says they're going to invade. The hawks in the Russian military will use the political weakness in Moscow to make their move. The timing would be right with the world distracted by the events in Moscow; few would dare protest a land grab by the Russian army."

"What will our Government do?"

"Nothing!"

That's not what I was expecting to hear, Andy thought, *not even a whimper?*

Winchester continued, "The last thing the current administration wants is adding fuel to the fire and appear to be taking sides by backing the hardliners, or seem to influence the hardliners by allowing them to topple the moderate regime of Yeltsin."

Yevenko arrived and waved at Andy as he placed his packed lunch in the refrigerator before he too reached for the coffee. Winchester nodded to Yevenko and resumed his conversation. "Andy, we've got two assets going over the border today. Kiev wants you to run them."

Andy nodded. *At last a breadcrumb ... now I can get on with the job they've sent me to do.*

"I'll get you the file," Winchester stood and headed over to the large gray wall safe. "If I remember correctly they are ornithologists." Andy looked puzzled for a moment.

"Bird watchers," Winchester said in a deliberately slow, raised voice.

"Oh, right ... I guess it gives them a cover for moving around the area with binoculars and long range cameras."

"Exactly." Winchester handed over the file and looked at his watch, "Study it quickly. You meet them in two hours at the cafe opposite the bus terminal in town."

Andy knew the bus terminal, just one block away and less than a two-minute walk. "Thanks, I'll get on with it now." He stood with his coffee and took himself and the file to a chair in a corner of the office to read about the husband and wife team he would be meeting that morning.

He found out that the Schwartz's mission would be to gather further evidence of the Russian troop build-up and identify which units were involved. Langley would use the information to work out the Russian military capability and from that the potential intent and objectives. Knowing which units were involved also told them who their commanders were likely to be and this, together with Langley's extensive database, would reveal how those commanders tended to direct formations and the tactics they would employ.

CHAPTER 5

The waitress placed Andy's coffee on the table next to a book on native European birds, just as an elderly couple, dressed in outdoor clothing and carrying small daypacks entered the cafe – Erik and Grunhilda Schwartz – he recognized them immediately. Erik was holding a camera tripod in his right hand. He watched as they scanned the room looking for their clue and, on seeing the book, they headed over to him.

"I see from your book, you're a like-minded friend. Are you a twitcher?" Erik asked.

"Yes. I'm looking for a Northern Goshawk. What are you looking for?" *The introductions were going as planned. The authentication had been positive so far.*

"We hope to see the European Honey Buzzard. We heard there have been sightings just across the border."

All good. Now onto business. "How long will you be looking for the Honey Buzzard?"

"Two days and then we'll be back out. We don't get much annual leave, so we can't commit much time," Grunhilda replied, "we'll call our children when we are out, to let them know we're safe."

"That makes sense. Do you have a good camera to capture the images of the Honey Buzzard?"

"Yes, complete with telephoto lens and a tripod." Erik held up the tripod as Andy sipped his coffee.

"Do you have a car?"

"No. We travel everywhere on public transport and we'll walk and hitch-hike to get to where we need to be. In twenty minutes we're taking the bus to Millerovo." Andy felt uneasy, *Shit! If they attract attention to themselves, they have no means of escape or the ability to move out of the area quickly.*

"You have a great time looking for the Honey Buzzard ... and be careful."

"We always are," Erik replied.

The couple headed to the counter where they picked up a breakfast menu. After placing their order, the couple chose a table away from Andy. Andy casually looked around the café and didn't detect anyone watching him or them. No one had entered the café since the assets had walked in, *So far, so good.*

Andy placed a 100,000 Karbovanets note on the table as a tip for the waitress. Then he headed for the door without a second glance at the assets. He made his way back to his apartment and the battered Skoda the team had procured for him. The car had peeling paint and bare wires for a stereo, but Andy felt confident nobody would want to steal it. Mechanically, the car was sound, on turning the key the engine fired immediately and ran smooth, however, the same couldn't be said for the exhaust which had an annoying rattle every time he revved the engine.

Andy drove on the deserted P22 heading North East out of town towards the border crossing with Russia. A large car park at the border post gave him a clear view of the crossing. He checked his watch. The Schwartz's bus would be arriving in half-an-hour. To pass the time Andy removed a pair of binoculars from the glove compartment and used them to carefully study the border post and the surrounding area.

The Ukrainian guards looked bored as they gave a cursory check on the passports of those arriving from Russia before waving them through. They made little effort to check those leaving the

Ukraine. Andy switched his attention to the Russian side of the border. There appeared to be three times the number of guards and, to one side, there was a watch a tower within which a heavy caliber machine gun covered the crossing. The Russian guards were more diligent in their duty, stopping and checking the papers of every person on foot; pulling over and searching one in three vehicles leaving; and, in contrast, searching every vehicle and taking twice as long checking paperwork of those entering Russia.

Looking just outside of the border posts he noted there were no barriers or fencing to mark the physical border, or restrict movement, between the two countries, just a mix of open farmland and forest. Andy looked further into Russia and could just make out, above the tree line, the metal roofing of the barrack blocks. He counted five larger structures which, from the intelligence satellites photos he'd seen, were large enough to conceal a regiment of main battle tanks, armored personnel carriers and supporting infantry.

A white van approaching the border from the Russian side caught his attention, as it performed a U-turn, bringing his focus back to the border post. Andy trained his binoculars on the two men who'd climbed out from the van and approached the guards. The first man, the driver, had a shaved head and took the lead. The van's passenger stood further back and kept out of the conversation.

Andy watched as they conversed for a few minutes and drew in three more border guards. He watched as the senior border guard saluted the shaved headed van driver. *What the hell?* Then the driver with his passenger returned to their van and waited. *The bus to Millerovo with the Schwartz's will be here soon.* Sure enough, less than five minutes later the battered bus for Millerovo lurched into view.

The only thing keeping the sixties vehicle on the road was an excellent garage mechanic and generous bribes to the local Ministry of Transportation vehicle inspectors. The bus pulled to a halt at the Ukrainian checkpoint. The bus doors opened and a single Ukrainian guard climbed on board.

Andy focused on the small group of passengers on the bus and, within seconds, picked out the Schwartz's. He watched as the guard quickly moved down the bus examining the passengers' passports. Less than a minute later the guard exited the bus and waved to the driver to move on. The bus slowly approached the Russian checkpoint and pulled to a halt at a metal barrier and road spikes.

Two Russian guards climbed on board and, moments later, all the passengers left the coach. They were directed to a single-story cinder block building with a red tin roof. After several minutes of apparent inactivity, one by one the passengers were released and directed to return to their transport. He checked each of the faces leaving the building. The Schwartz's entered the building as passengers four and five. The Schwartz's were still inside as passengers eight and nine had left. *Where are they? What's taking so long? Shit!* Andy was on high alert now but knew, if something had happened to them, there was absolutely nothing he could do to help them without causing a major incident.

After what felt like an eternity, the smiling faces of the Schwartz's appeared as they headed back to their seats on the bus. Being the last passengers to leave the building, they were followed by a guard who turned and signaled to the driver of the van. The road spikes were pulled clear and the barrier raised allowing the coach to slowly pull away from the border crossing. The Schwartz's were now in hostile territory. *Good luck. I'll see you in forty-eight hours.*

Then just as the bus went passed, Andy saw the white van move off, he wasn't sure that it was actually following the bus, but he felt uneasy after what had transpired earlier with the border guards saluting the driver ... *this doesn't look right.* With nothing to be done he put the car in gear and went home to wait it out and get some sleep.

CHAPTER 6

Forty-seven hours later Andy was back at the crossing waiting for the bus from Millerovo to return. This time he brought a thermos flask of coffee from the office to make his wait a touch more comfortable. Fine rain was falling, making him look through the rain streaked glass of his Skoda. His range of visibility increased and decreased as the rain eased and intensified, bringing the border post and the guards on both sides in and out of view. He checked the time on his black plastic Casio digital watch.

Any time now, he told himself, as he used the binoculars to scan the approach road to the Russian side of the border. *Nothing*. He cast his gaze over the machine gun position in the tower. One of the two guards in the tower had trained their powerful binoculars on him, the other held a radio to his mouth. Andy was fully alert, *Damn!* He knew attracting their attention wasn't great but he had to wait this out; if he moved now it would look more suspicious than if he stayed put, so he waited.

Movement along the approach road made Andy switched his focus to the approaching bus which slowed as it neared the Russian checkpoint and pulled to a stop at the barrier. Two guards went on board and moments later the passengers streamed off one by one and made their way towards the cinder block hut. The guards exited the coach, indicating there were no more passengers. Andy adjusted the focus back to the passengers; the Schwartz's were not among them ... *No, no, no, where are they*? He felt the color drain from his face.

"Where are the Schwartz's?" he said to himself. *I can't have lost the assets from my first run,* he thought.

A few minutes later, the passengers started to exit the hut, one at a time, returning to their seats on the dry, warm bus. Once the last passenger had retaken their seat, the bus doors closed, the road spikes were pulled clear and the barrier rose allowing the bus to drive through to the Ukrainian side of the border where two bored-looking guards waved it to stop. The doors opened and one of the guards got onboard to check each passenger's passport. Satisfied he stepped off the bus, turned to face the driver and waved him on. The bus doors closed as it pulled away and headed into the Ukraine ... back to Luhansk.

Andy reminded himself there were two coaches per day from Millerovo and the next one would be through the checkpoint in six hours. It was unusual, but not exceptional, for assets to miss their agreed rendezvous and, when public transport formed part of the plan, disruptions should always be expected. Andy knew if the Schwartz's missed their bus they'd catch the next one, he'd just have to come back later ... *So much for making a good impression!*

He started the engine, set his wipers to clear the windscreen and headed back to the station. A few minutes later he overtook the bus he'd been so keen to meet and twenty minutes later walked into the field station.

"You're back quickly. Shouldn't you be debriefing your assets?" Kowalski called out as Andy threw his car keys onto the shared table.

"They didn't cross," Andy replied, trying to keep calm and appear unphased.

"What?" Kowalski sat up straight and started to listen intently.

"It was a no show. I'll go back when the next bus is due." Andy went to the kitchen area and standing next to the sink opened the thermos flask and rinsed out the dregs of the stale coffee.

"Any calls to the emergency number?"

"No one has called," Kowalski replied.

"Any indicators that something has happened to them?" Andy asked as he placed the flask, its cap and cup onto the draining board, he felt resigned to their fate.

"Nothing. It's been quiet, apart from the increased radio traffic on the Russian military frequencies."

"Do you mind if I take your car when I head back this afternoon? The Russians took too much interest in mine this time, so probably not a good thing to show up in it again!"

"Sure," Kowalski threw his keys to Andy, "it's the dark blue BMW parked across the street."

"Thanks. I've got another asset crossing tomorrow, I'll see if I can use Winchester's motorcycle tomorrow."

Kowalski laughed, "There is more chance of you finding rocking horse shit than him giving up the keys to his beloved Kawasaki sports bike."

Andy held up Kowalski's keys. "In the meantime I have your car!"

Yevenko called out, "Hey don't lose that asset too!" He started laughing with Kowalski. Andy relaxed a bit … *these guys are ok!*

"Cut it out guys," he was enjoying the banter, "the Schwartz's will turn up in a few hours … I hope!"

Andy sat and started to read the file on his next asset scheduled to make the crossing. The Schwartz's absence gave him a headache. Without their information it would be difficult to direct the next asset to make full use of their limited time in Russia. The Schwartz's were to have helped by providing data to assist with this assets targeting.

His new asset was Mikhail Stalinki, aged 32, born in Vladivostok, he was a business consultant who regularly traveled across the region advising small businesses on how to improve their productivity and access Government grants. Stalinki spent five days every few weeks in Russia gathering intelligence for the agency whilst going about his business. He had become a reliable asset who acted cautiously and avoided all unnecessary risks.

Stalinki had a photographic memory, and was clearly a bright guy, with a degree in Economics from Moscow State University and a Masters from the Berlin Institute of Technology, but Andy had to search through the file to find Stalinki's motivation for helping the agency. He found it on page six. Stalinki wanted to move to America and needed a Green Card to get in. His recruiter had offered him the chance of getting one, with a firm recommendation from the agency, once he proved himself and helped the agency.

Four hours later Andy refilled the thermos flask with hot coffee and signed-out a pair of powerful binoculars before heading out to Kowalski's car which Andy couldn't help notice had a powerful engine and a top of the line stereo system which played loud rock music. Compared to driving his Skoda, the BMW accelerated with ease, stuck to the road like its tires were coated with glue and its engine purred when he pressed his foot on the gas. The border crossing looked quiet and much the same as earlier in the day when Andy pulled into the car park. He switched off the engine, waited for a few minutes and checked his digital watch. *The coach will be here in ten minutes.* Andy opened the flask and poured himself a coffee. He took a sip and immediately grimaced as the liquid burnt his mouth. He swallowed the hot drink and felt it going down his throat, his eyes watered through discomfort. Andy put the steaming coffee cup down onto the cars dashboard and carefully placed the flask in the passenger foot well before reaching for the binoculars.

With the rain having eased off, he had a good view of both sides of the border crossing. He panned over to the guard tower, the two guards were in position, however, this time they showed no interest in the BMW and appeared to be engaged in conversation. Andy swung his attention back to the checkpoint where a farm vehicle, loaded with produce, had just crossed from the Ukrainian side and had become the focus of the Russians. While the farmer went to the hut with his paperwork, three guards climbed into the back of the truck and were now carefully scrutinizing the sacks of carrots, potatoes and cabbages.

Two guards climbed down, leaving one guard alone, probably the most junior. Andy watched as he started to open the sacks and rummage inside to see if there was anything hidden. Even before he'd got through his third sack, he stopped, scratched his head, and looked around. He probably believed no one was watching as he put the sacks back and climbed down from the old truck before completing his task.

Andy saw the bus from Millerovo slowing as it approached the border post. He put the binoculars down as he watched the scene unfold. The farmer climbed back into his cab. A plume of oily black smoke erupted from the exhaust pipe as the truck pulled away making the guards take a few steps back and attempt to waft the choking smoke away with their hands. The bus had stopped and a guard had climbed on board. Andy picked up the binoculars and used them to watch the passengers disembark heading into the building for processing. There were fewer passengers than had been on the earlier coach and, once again, the Schwartz's weren't amongst them.

"What the hell is going on?" He said to himself. He now felt very concerned for the Schwartz's safety. *Another no show.* There was no point in sticking around, instead he fired up the engine and headed back to the field station. He switched the music off and drove in silence. He needed the quiet to consider the fate of the Schwartz's. If he could find out where they were, would he be able to help them? In the back of his mind, he knew the reality of their situation and he would just have to wait it out … they were on their own. *They knew the risks*, he tried to convince himself but it didn't sit easily and he felt he had failed them.

Walking into the field station, Yevenko's expression told Andy something had happened to the Schwartz's. "What's going on?" Andy asked as he approached the three CIA officers.

"We're getting reports, from the Russian police radio network, that two bodies have been found. They say an elderly couple had been shot and stripped of their valuables." Winchester replied.

"Another robbery gone wrong." Yevenko chipped in.

"What a coincidence!" Kowalski added.

"Any suspects?" Andy asked.

"None," Winchester replied, "you'll need to write it up, then send your report to Kiev and Langley. They'll need to know what's happened."

"Yeah, I know," his voice betraying the disappointment he felt at having failed in his first assignment.

CHAPTER 7

After a restless night's sleep and a light breakfast, Andy headed into the field station to check-in and grab a coffee. Andy read with interest the cables and reports which had come in overnight. Langley confirmed, via multiple sources that the Schwartz's had been murdered. Their bodies would be repatriated to Germany in a week or so. The reports said the police in Bonn had already broken the news to the Schwartz's two adult children who still lived in the city.

Next, Andy read an intercepted document from the Russian police which concluded the Schwartz's had found themselves in a dangerous part of town … their fine clothes and expensive camera equipment had attracted the wrong sort of attention; they'd been robbed and murdered. With his reading over, Andy headed into the equipment room and emerged with a high resolution digital camera together with a powerful telephoto lens.

"Yevenko, could I use your car? Mine and Kowalski's have been to the border recently and I'd rather not attract attention." Andy offered a warm, reassuring smile.

"Sure. It's the black Renault parked outside" Yevenko handed his car keys over to Andy continuing, "you may need to put some gas in it, the tank's a bit low."

"No problem." Andy headed to the door and as he reached the handle Winchester called out after him. "Hey, you be careful out there. Make sure you come back."

Andy turned and gave a brief wave, then opened the door and

headed downstairs to the sidewalk. *Winchester sounded genuinely concerned.* He easily found Yevenko's car and placed the camera on the passenger seat, then drove to the gas station and filled the tank as a way to repay Yevenko. He checked his watch and worked out he had twenty minutes to reach the rendezvous with Stalinki. *Plenty of time.*

Less than ten minutes later, Andy parked in the empty car park of a local art gallery. The two-story gray concrete building with a flat roof looked to be in need of urgent maintenance. *This place hadn't seen a lick of paint in decades.* Andy checked his watch. *I'm early.* He pushed the digital camera under the passenger seat to conceal it from view, got out of the car, locked it with the remote and headed into the gallery.

Inside, and in sharp contrast to the building's dilapidated exterior, the gallery was modern, uncluttered and well lit. It had polished concrete floors and each interior wall was painted a different pastel color which worked well with artwork being exhibited. Sculptures from local artisans were displayed in the large rooms with spot lighting showing their textures and subtle complexities. On the walls in one room were hung paintings, as Andy stepped into another room there were enlarged photographs, some color, most in black and white. If he didn't know his location, he could have believed he was standing in a gallery in Paris, New York or London.

Andy worked his way slowly through the deserted gallery to its cafe, which with its sleek industrial look, reminded him of a piece of art. A steel ribbed floor furnished with steel benches, tables and chairs and lit by six large polished-chrome lights hanging down on long cables from the ceiling. On the walls were positioned the blades from industrial fans, the silver heatproof head-cover from a steel worker's protective gear and, in the middle of one wall, a blown up color photograph. The photograph showed a steel worker recoiling away from lethal golden sparks as a large mechanical ladle, slung from an overhead crane, poured molten metal into a furnace. Andy immediately recognized Stalinki from his photograph in the file. Stalinki stood at the counter ordering a herbal tea and toast. Stalinki paid and found himself a table. Andy ordered a black coffee, paid and joined Stalinki.

"Have you been in this gallery before?" Andy asked.

"Yes, this is my third visit. It never ceases to impress me. Each time it is different."

The authentication process is going well. "What's your favorite piece?"

"I haven't seen it today. I think they've sold it."

Andy smiled and offered Stalinki his hand. "Good to meet you Mikhail."

Stalinki smiled in return. "What do you want me to focus on while I'm in Russia?"

This guy is straight to the point. "There's a build-up of Russian forces around Millerovo. We'd like to know which units have been deployed and gather any clues as to how ready they are to move."

"How will I know that?" Stalinki asked. They fell silent as the young waitress arrived with Stalinki's herbal tea, toast, butter and preserves. She carefully placed the items on their table and made eye contact with Andy, holding his gaze for an extra second, then left the two men alone.

"Look for clues, for example, are the soldiers undertaking maintenance tasks on their armored vehicles, if so, have they got engines out and tracks off, or are they just tightening wheel nuts and adding oil to the engines. Are they wearing full combat uniform with helmets or are they relaxing in mixed uniform or undertaking physical training or sports. That sort of thing."

"Okay, I get it." Stalinki replied. "Do you need photographs and video evidence?"

Andy thought about the Schwartz's and their photographic approach. "No, don't do anything to draw attention to yourself, just remember what you can. Take time to speak with the locals. Listen to conversations in the bars, nightclubs and restaurants. If you see something, make a coded reference to it so you can recall it later. If it feels unsafe, cut your visit short and get back this side of the border."

"I'm a good photographer. I've taken pictures before," Stalinki protested.

"Mikhail, I don't want you taking any unnecessary risks," he looked Stalinki in the eye and lied, "You're too important to us. I don't want you to get picked up with a camera so close to Russian military formations."

Stalinki puffed out his chest and with both hands pulled down and straightened the front of his jacket. The conversation paused as the waitress arrived with Andy's coffee. She placed the coffee down on the table in front of him, her hand gently brushed against his as she moved away. He glanced up and noticed the waitress looking down at him for a few seconds. She smiled, turned and left the two of them.

Stalinki started eating his toast. "I've not seen you before. Are you new to the team?"

Andy wasn't here to make friends with Stalinki, "I'm here for a few weeks to fill in."

"Where are you from, Mr...?"

Mikhail is really fishing for something about me. "My name is Flint. You don't need to know any more." He sipped his coffee and frowned. It tasted more of chicory than coffee. *Definitely not to my taste.* He pushed his near full cup away. "I'll watch you cross at the border. Don't acknowledge me. I'll next see you on your return and debrief you."

"Okay."

Andy stood and headed for the exit. When he reached the door the waitress approached and pushed a piece of paper into his hand. Andy looked at the slip of paper and saw a phone number written in blue ink. Andy faced her and smiled. He saw her giggle and felt himself blush. Andy thanked her and headed for the Renault.

Twenty minutes later he pulled into the car park at the border crossing. It looked unchanged from his previous visits with only a handful of people making the crossing. "Damn! I never asked what car he drove and he hadn't parked at the art gallery," he said to himself as he reached down for the camera. The powerful lens gave a magnification many times better than the binoculars he'd been using. He picked an object, the guard tower and zoomed in. Even at this distance he could read the insignia on the guard's uniforms and see the bullets in the ammunition belt which fed into the heavy machine gun.

Andy changed his point of interest to the hut and zoomed out so he could fit the whole building into his viewfinder as he did so a silver BMW and a motorcycle parked outside the hut came into view. While Andy didn't know much about motorcycles, this one had a powerful looking engine, a fat back tire and raised, wide handlebars. This was a chopper. To test the camera, he took a picture of the motorcycle then switched the cameras mode so he could look at the image he'd just taken. Using the camera's controls Andy zoomed in and scrolled right, enlarging the manufactures logo on the side of the gas tank to fill the entire display. Then his attention was grabbed by a man wearing motorcycle leathers and carrying a black helmet emerging from the hut. Andy switched the camera's mode to take photographs and peered at the man through the camera's view finder.

He looks familiar ... where have I seen him before? Andy snapped three photographs in rapid succession of the man and, when he played them back his memory was nudged to remember ... he was the guy with the shaved-head driver of the white van the day the Schwartz's crossed the border. *What's he doing back at the border?* The mystery man sat on the motorcycle, lit a cigarette and watched the border crossing from close up. Andy noticed the guards paid him no attention. Ten minutes later a dark blue, new edition Audi was waved through the Ukrainian checkpoint and stopped at the barrier on the Russian side. Andy zoomed in on the Audi and took a picture of the rear capturing the image of a red sticker in the rear window and a long white scratch on the bumper. A Russian guard approached the driver's window for a brief exchange, moments later Stalinki climbed from the car carrying his Russian passport and some paperwork in his hands.

Andy took two photographs of Stalinki as he approached the hut. After a few minutes Stalinki reemerged and appeared to be smiling. Andy zoomed out and could see the man on the motorcycle also watching Stalinki. *Now why are you so interested in him?* Andy captured the scene in crystal clear, high resolution, digital wizardry. He lowered the camera down and surveyed the wider scene. Everything looked normal. Stalinki had returned to his car and started his engine. The guards removed the road spikes and raised the barrier. Moments later Stalinki drove away from the Ukraine and deeper into Russia.

Andy turned his attention back to the man on the motorcycle. The tip of the cigarette grew brighter as the man took a long draw on it. He removed the cigarette from his mouth and flicked the butt onto the road, where bright sparks erupted as it landed. As the motorcyclist looked around, Andy raised the camera and was able to snap a good picture of the man's face before it disappeared into his helmet. Andy watched him fire up his bike and rev the engine. Its distinctive deep throated growl was loud even at this distance. The chopper accelerated away with roar as it chased after the Audi. The border guards replaced the road spikes and lowered the road barrier. It dawned on Andy the guards manning the road spikes and barrier had left the crossing open after Stalinki drove through, as though they knew the man with the motorcycle would follow after the Audi. *Great ... looks like I'm about to lose my third asset.*

Andy felt curious about the mysterious motorcyclist and wondered about the man's identity as he drove back to the field station in Luhansk. He parked Yevenko's Renault against the sidewalk outside the office, headed inside and up the stairs with the camera in hand. Before he reached the door handle, Andy heard the lock give an electronic buzz as the mechanism released.
Someone's paying attention with the cameras. He pushed hard against the heavy door and entered the main office. Yevenko stepped away from the monitors which displayed the live camera feeds and looked at Andy. Andy threw the keys to the Renault at Yevenko. "It's now got a full tank."

"Thanks."

Andy headed over to one of the workstations and placed the camera on the table next to it. Once logged in, he removed the 2GB memory card from the camera and inserted it into the workstation. The automatic virus scan kicked in and started checking the integrity and payload of the memory card. After a few minutes the screen on the workstation displayed a new icon – a green tick – meaning Andy didn't have to destroy the memory card.

He quickly typed up an email in which he said a *'person of interest'* had been at the border when the Schwartz's crossed and again when Stalinki crossed. Finally, he attached all of the images of the motorcyclist and hit *'Send'*. With the email sent to Langley and copied into the Head of the Ukrainian desk at the Embassy in Kiev, Andy moved onto his personal emails.

One message jumped out at him and made him smile. He immediately opened the email from Lenya. She'd used the booking agency Andy had provided and her flights were arranged and she'd be arriving late morning in two days and staying for a week. Andy typed and sent his reply in which he said he was looking forward to seeing her, spending time being shown around the area and meeting her wider family including uncle Vanya. *I'm going to have to clean the apartment, maybe invest in a vacuum cleaner.* He logged into the agency's HR system and requested the five days' vacation and sent the request off.

CHAPTER 8

Two days later, the day started much like any other for Andy when he arrived at the field station. He'd planned to work for an hour before heading over to the Severodonetsk airport a two-hour drive to pick up Lenya. He felt excited about seeing her and hoped his leave request had been approved. He powered up his workstation, then logged in to check through the overnight communications and, much to his relief, he read that his request for annual leave had been approved.

He read a report which stated that the high level of radio traffic from just across the border had continued. The analysts in Langley had deduced from the call signs and chatter from the multiple networks that the military buildup had continued at a pace. Satellite imagery showed the Russian naval base at Sevastopol on the Black Sea had also seen major reinforcements arrive over the last few days. The intelligence picture indicated a high probability of a military invasion of the Ukraine across multiple fronts to seize all of the Russian speaking areas, including the Crimea.

Andy moved onto the next report which said the police in Millerovo had found the body of Mikhail Stalinki on the city dump. Andy felt light headed as the color drained from his face. He ran his right hand through his hair and forced himself to breath slowly before he re-read the report. *They've murdered Stalinki. The loss of two assets was bad. The loss of a third is catastrophic.*

"Are you okay? You don't look too good," Winchester called out.

"My asset, Mikhail Stalinki ... has been murdered!" the other agents stopped what they were doing and looked towards Andy.

"Shit! We have a serious problem. We had some earlier assets get themselves murdered, then Lynch, the Schwartz's and now Stalinki." Kowalski announced to the room.

"I'm going over to Millerovo to see what I can find out." Andy added.

"Hold on Andy, we need to get this cleared by Langley before you go running around Russia," Winchester said as he tried to reign Andy back.

"Maybe getting things cleared by Langley is what's getting these people killed. After all, it seems someone is tipping off the bad guys as to when, where and who, we have crossing. The Schwartz's and Stalinki were followed from the moment they crossed the border. I saw a shaved-head guy who was somehow involved … it was odd that one of the border guards saluted him. Then his sidekick turned up on a motorbike yesterday. These guys were already waiting. They knew we had assets crossing and they dealt with them … permanently."

Kowalski added: "This sounds bad. I agree with Andy, someone should go across and learn what they can about the murders. We will report back to Langley afterwards … no point giving the game away while we gather intel. At this rate we'll lose more assets and we can't afford to do that unchecked. Nikolai, you still got that contact at Vendispanser Hospital?"

"Yes I have. She's a doctor there. I'm sure she'll help," Yevenko replied. "I'll head over to the public phone booth and call her." Yevenko grabbed his jacket and headed out of the door.

Andy poured himself a strong coffee. "Anyone else?" he asked as he turned to the room.

"Sure, two sugars," answered Winchester. Andy reached for a cup for Winchester and poured him a black coffee, then stirred two generous teaspoons of sugar. Andy walked over to Winchester and handed him his coffee, then headed for one of the workstations.

"Has anyone read anything about the query I made regarding the identity of the man on the motorcycle?" Winchester and Kowalski shook their heads. "I'll check to see if anything has come in." Andy fired up the workstation, logged in and started checking for messages in reply to his query. *Nothing. Not even an acknowledgment to confirm they'd received it.* Andy started to check the office email account, then moved onto its archived mail and deleted folders without any success. As he logged out of the workstation Yevenko returned.

"I spoke with my contact at the hospital. She's on shift this morning and agreed to help find where your murdered friend has been taken."

"My murdered friend." Andy replied as he headed to the safe to retrieve his German issued passport with the alias Manfred Vessler.

"Yes. I couldn't say he was an agency asset who you'd met only once. If I did that, she'd have hung up. So he's an old friend who you've known for years and kept in touch with. You've come out here to spend time with him and before you met up, you've heard the terrible news that he's been murdered. You can't believe it and need to see him for yourself before you tell his family of the tragic news." *This guy is teaching me how to suck eggs!*

"What is she to you and this office?" Andy asked.

"Just over a year ago, I'd been inside the Millerovo Airbase when a security patrol disturbed me and we ended up in a fire fight. I took a round in my left arm, they were not so lucky and I escaped. I was bleeding badly and I couldn't stop the blood loss. Anyway, long story short, I crashed my car and she found me. Took me to hospital and patched me up. Tatyana kept me off the books and out of the system. She saved my life. That's what she is to me."

"Thanks for the context. Morgan, you're going to hate me for asking, but I've been to the border in each of our cars and must ask whether I can use your car?" Andy already knew the answer, Winchester didn't have a car … he rode a powerful Kawasaki sports bike … his pride and joy. Winchester didn't look impressed at Andy's request.

"Have you a license to ride a bike?" the tone had that sense of resignation as if he knew the answer before he had asked the question but hoped the answer would still be a big 'no'.

"Yes."

"Have you passed your bike test?"

"Yes."

"You ever ridden a sports bike before?"

"Yes. My brother had a Suzuki RGV," he lied. Andy had only once ridden a Yamaha 125 and it certainly wasn't a sports bike.

"You sure you can handle it?"

"Come on. Yes, or no! I'll bring it back with a full tank of gas and I'll even clean it for you at the weekend."

Winchester realized he wasn't going to win this exchange, "Sure." he threw the keys to Andy, "Helmet is over there," Winchester added as he pointed to the coat stand where there was a black helmet, with the image of a flaming dragon. "Let it warm up for the first ten minutes before you open it up."

"Okay. I heard you. I'll go easy."

"Use my leather jacket, it might be a bit big on you, but better than nothing if you do come off."

"Thanks." As Andy headed for Winchester's jacket and helmet,

Yevenko approached.

"Her name is Tatyana Skolkovich. She works in the neurology department at the Vendispanser Hospital."

"Can you describe her to me?"

"Shorter than you and quite thin. Brown eyes and hair which she tends to have braided. She usually wears casual tops, pants and sneakers for work and, always, a fine gold necklace with a gold locket. She's thirty-two, but looks older."

"Can you tell me something personal about her?"

"She was born outside Moscow, has two sisters, she's the oldest and her favorite color is green."
"Thanks." Andy donned Winchesters leather jacket and grabbed his helmet. *Lenya. Crap! I need to pick her up at 11 from the airport.* He'd got caught up in the moment and forgot his commitment to her. "Hey guys. Can I ask a big favor? My girlfriend Lenya arrives on the morning flight from Moscow and I was to pick up her up from Severodonetsk airport, can one of you pick her up and then drop her off at my apartment?" He held up his apartment keys which were attached to his car keys.

"Yeah, sure," Kowalski called out, "I'll do it."

"Thanks. I know I should pick her up, but I need to find out more about Stalinki's murder. Tell her I'm sorry I couldn't pick her up. But give her the good news that I have the rest of the week off work to spend time with her and I'll make it up to her." Andy grabbed a black marker board pen and wrote down her name on a piece of white paper and handed the paper and keys over to Kowalski before he headed to the door.

***

Andy took extreme caution riding Winchester's motorcycle to the border. He kept to the speed limit and didn't accelerate too quickly when coming out of bends. Even at relatively slow speeds he felt the bike wanted to race and power through the bends. Arriving at the border post, the Ukrainian guards waved him through while the Russian guards stopped him and indicated he needed to park outside the hut. Two guards approached and asked to see his passport. After closely examining his German passport for several seconds, they ordered him to take his helmet off and as a final check they compared the photograph in the passport against his likeness, before returning his passport and ordering him to go into the hut. Andy climbed off the bike and, with his passport in hand, entered the hut.

Inside he faced an elevated counter which forced him to look up at the border official.

"Passport!" The official demanded. Andy handed his passport over. *This is a bit pointless!* He thought as he had assumed if there was a problem with his papers the guards outside would have already detained him.

"German?"

"Yes."

"Where you go?" The official started looking at his passport.

"I just want to go into Russia for the day as I'm so close ... to find out if it as different as I've been told."

"Where will you be staying?"

"I'm staying in Luhansk. All my things are there as I don't plan to stay overnight; I will go back to my hotel in Luhansk later tonight."

The official waved Andy's passport at him. "No visa."

"No. I'm sorry. This was kind of a spur of the moment thing. Can I get a visa here?" He knew he could for a hundred US dollars.

The official smiled. "Yes, of course. You can pay in Russian Rubles, Ukrainian Karbovanets, United States Dollars or a credit card." Andy reached for his wallet and touched his credit card, immediately realizing the cards were in the name Andy Flint and not Manfred Vessler. Then let his fingers reach deeper as he removed a wad of notes.

The border official appeared happy when he saw the money. "Cash is very good. American Dollars perfect." Andy knew he was about to be fleeced, but if it got him over the border, it would be worth it! The official rubbed his hands together. *Here it comes ...* "Two hundred American Dollars please." Andy very deliberately counted out the twenty dollar bills, one at a time, placing each note carefully on the counter one on top of the other.

When Andy had finished counting, the official scooped up the notes and counted them himself to be certain he'd not been cheated by a sleight of hand. Satisfied, the official stamped Andy's passport and slid it back. He then pushed a customs declaration form for Andy to complete. Andy counted the remaining cash in his wallet, filled in the form and signed and dated the declaration. The official cast a cursory glance at the form before he stamped it and handed it back. "Your visa is for twenty-four hours. Welcome to Russia, Mr. Vessler."

Andy headed outside, jumped on Winchester's bike. During the ride away from the border crossing his confidence on handling the powerful machine grew and on the straight sections along the empty highway he fought the constant temptation to open the throttle. *I don't want to draw any attention to myself.* Thirty minutes later he pulled into the car park at Vendispanser Hospital. He found a parking space, flicked the stand with his foot and turned off the ignition then, with helmet in hand, he headed for the main entrance.

The woman at the reception desk looked old and beyond her working age. Andy could see a Communist Party badge pinned to the lapel of her hand knitted green top. She looked up at Andy with a bored expression. "How may I help you today?" she asked as her eyes carefully studied Andy.

"I'm here to see Doctor Skolkovich." Andy replied with a friendly smile.

"Patients that way," she said pointing a gnarly index finger towards a sign which read '*Day Patient Appointments*', an arrow indicating the direction down a corridor off to the right.

"Sorry, no, I'm not a patient," Andy said, "she's expecting me." The receptionist gave him a look of disapproval and then used her primitive bulky computer to page Dr. Skolkovich. Andy didn't need to wait long for her to arrive.

"Manfred, I'm Dr. Skolkovich, thank you for coming, I'm so sorry about your friend." She matched the description given by Yevenko right down to the fine gold necklace around her neck. She held out her hand for Andy, which he shook firmly, "I made inquiries and I found that your friend is at rest here in our morgue."

"Thank you. Can I see him?" he asked politely.

Dr. Skolkovich nodded, turned and headed down the corridor the receptionist had indicated moments earlier. Andy quickly followed her, when they reached the hospital elevators she stopped and pressed the button to summon the elevator. The doors opened with a shudder. *That's not a good sign ... I really don't like these small metal boxes.* Once they were both inside she hit the button marked *Morgue.* The doors closed and they began their descent into the building's lower levels.

Arriving in the basement, the doors opened again with a bit of a shudder. Stepping into the corridor, a short fat man dressed in green hospital scrubs approached them, the morgue's bright lighting reflected off his shiny bald head. "Dr. Skolkovich, the body is ready for you."

He led them into the visitor's viewing area, a bland room with a large dark purple curtain along one wall. The technician pulled the cord to open the curtain, revealing a window which overlooked a metal table upon which the body of Mikhail Stalinki had been rested. Stalinki's body was covered in a white sheet which had been pulled up to his shoulders. Andy approached the window and looked closely at Stalinki's waxy complexion.

"That's my friend Mikhail." He wiped an imaginary tear from his eyes and sniffed. "How did he die?"

"He was shot in the back of the head at close range." The technician replied in a matter of fact manner. "He died instantly and would not have felt a thing."

Wow! Mr. Empathy here really knows how to break bad news, Andy thought.

Dr. Skolkovich looked horrified and gave an angry stare at the technician. "I'm very sorry for my colleague's directness. Your friend died quickly and under unusual circumstances. He wouldn't have felt any pain."

"That's dreadful. Absolutely dreadful." Andy removed a handkerchief and blew his nose. Then made a point of wiping his eyes. "Apart from being shot did you find anything else?"

The technician looked across at the doctor, then back at Andy. "Apart from his personal effects, I found something in his jacket pocket, I thought it was unusual, it may mean something more to you."

"Go on." Andy prompted him.

The technician walked out of the visitor's room and into the examination area. Andy watched him through the window as the technician reached for a small, clear plastic box which appeared to hold Stalinki's personal possessions. The technician rummaged around for a moment before he stopped and then reached for an item before returning to the visitor's room with it.

"This is what I found" the technician handed over a small piece of green card.

CHAPTER 9

"How was Millerovo?" Kowalski called out as Andy entered the CIA station. Andy placed Winchester's helmet on the coat stand while he still wore Winchester's leather jacket.

"There's a problem," the three other agents looked at Andy. Winchester looked pale. "Hey, it's not about your bike. It's still in one piece and has a full tank of gas." Winchester relaxed. "I've got to go and take a leak, I'll tell you about the problem when I return." He headed towards the bathroom when at the last moment he called out to Kowalski, "Is Lenya at my apartment?"

"Yes, though she was very annoyed you weren't there to meet her. I think she'd calmed down by the time I dropped her off. She's waiting for you."

"Great. Thanks. I really appreciate your help." Andy entered the bathroom and locked the cubicle door. He lifted the lid on the toilet seat and reached for his belt buckle but stopped when he heard the distinctive deep throated roar of a big motorcycle being ridden away. But this motorcycle sounded familiar and it wasn't Kowalski's. *That's the bike from the border crossing. What's it doing here?*

Much later, when he tried to recall what happened, Andy wasn't sure on the exact sequence of events. Whether he heard the explosion before or after the room went dark and the floor disintegrated below him, he couldn't be certain. One moment he was standing in the bathroom. The next, he lay buried under rubble. It was dark. His ears ringing from the explosion.

He felt pain in his lower legs. He moved his hands down his legs and felt something pinning his legs down. It was the ceramic hand basin which he confirmed when his right hand brushed against the tap that was still attached. Using both hands he grabbed the hand basin and lifted it up so his legs were free and felt the flow of blood restored. With the pain from his legs easing off, Andy ran his hands through his hair, it felt wet. *Is that blood or water?* He moved his hands around his skull and pressed down at various points to feel for injuries.

Nothing. I'm a lucky man. The whole building must have come down. I need to get out.

Enveloped in darkness, Andy felt around him to build up a picture of the space within which he was trapped. He appeared to be in a small air pocket in which he could sit up. "Help! Is there anyone out there? Help!" he shouted. He heard no response. "Guys, I'm trapped in here." Still nothing. He couldn't be completely sure if anyone had responded as his ears were still ringing from the explosion.

He decided he needed to try and free himself. He wiped the dirt out from his eyes and looking around, saw a pin prick of light over his right shoulder. He shuffled around and rested on his right side to face the faint glimmer of light. Andy started to move the rubble from the area where the light originated to the space where his feet were, then pushed the rubble further away with his feet. Soon his hand broke free of his tomb allowing more light to spill over him and he could feel a fresh breeze on his skin.

"I'm getting out of here," he said to himself. Then as loud as he could, he shouted. "Help!" He waved his hand through the hole he'd just made. Andy could hear shouting and footsteps clambering over the wreckage towards him. "I'm here. Help!"

"Here! … someone's here … this one's alive! Come on! Get over here!" A voice urgently called out. He could hear his rescuers working together lifting and discarding the rubble which had buried him. Soon, the bright daylight blinded him, making him blink repeatedly until his eyes adjusted to the light. He felt strong hands gripping his shoulders, arms, waist and legs. Moments later they were lifting him out of his temporary tomb and placed him onto a stretcher.

"How many of you were in the office?" he heard a woman's voice ask. Andy turned his head to look up at the woman who asked the question; her uniform told him she was a police officer.

"There were three others. Have you found them?"

He watched her expression harden, then she turned to the rescuers, "Okay, you can ease it off. There are no more people to find. Everyone's accounted for."

"My colleagues. How are they?" Andy asked.

"They're dead. You are the only survivor." Andy felt his world closing in on him. He felt dizzy. He needed to get back into the present and forced himself to breath slowly and deeply. He looked at his body to see if he carried any obvious injuries as a rescuer placed a blanket over him. Two men lifted the stretcher and carefully found their footing as they stepped over the rubble. The police officer stayed by Andy's side.

"Can you tell me what happened?" he asked the officer.

"I think the restaurant had a gas explosion. It leveled the entire building. We've seen gas explosions before, it's nothing new to us."

Once clear of the debris, they gently lowered the stretcher to the ground. They were close to a growing crowd of ghoulish onlookers.

"We'll get you to hospital where we'll take your statement, then you'll need to formally identify the bodies of your colleagues. In the meantime, I need to tape the area off and keep people out until we've examined the scene in detail."

"Thanks, Officer." Andy replied. Apart from the weapons which they had locked in the gun safe, he knew that the police wouldn't find anything of significance … all their systems were designed to wipe everything and self-destruct the moment there was an incursion.

"An ambulance is on its way," the officer said to Andy. Then she spoke to the two men who'd carried the stretcher. "You two. Come with me to help tape the area off."

They left Andy alone trying to make sense of what had happened. He didn't know how much time had elapsed since the explosion and couldn't rule out that he had been knocked out for a while. *I don't think I'm injured. I don't need to go to hospital. I need to let the Embassy know what happened and get a message to Langley.*

Andy checked his pockets. He still had his German passport, his wallet and Winchester's motorcycle keys. He glanced across at the police officer who appeared busy getting the area cordoned off and preventing anyone removing evidence. She wasn't looking in his direction. Andy pulled the woolen blanket away, got to his feet and made his way slowly towards the crowd of onlookers. Moments later he was amongst the crowd, in less than thirty meters he was clear of them and on his way to his apartment.

CHAPTER 10

He'd left that morning with only one set of keys, and they'd been given to Lenya, so Andy had to knock on his apartment door hoping she hadn't gone out to explore. He didn't have to wait long for her to open the door. Her warm smile made his heart skip a beat then, seeing him in torn clothing and covered in dirt with blood and cuts covering his face and hands, her expression changed to horror and she threw her arms around him. He winced!

"What happened?" but before he could answer she placed a kiss square on his lips.

When she broke away he answered. "There was an explosion at the office. The building came down with me in it. The police think it was a gas explosion from the restaurant below us."

"How's Kowalski and the others?" She released Andy from her embrace and led him into the apartment.

Andy shook his head. "No one else made it."

She cradled her face in both hands looking shocked: "That's awful, you need to let your main office know what's happened so they can tell their families ... but first let me clean you up and check that you haven't been seriously hurt." Andy knew better than to argue with Lenya. The calls to Langley and Kiev could wait another ten minutes. He sat on the settee. "Where's your first aid kit? You do have one?" she asked.

The agency provided each field agent with a comprehensive medical pack which could treat anything up to major surgery complete with sterile instruments, surgical dressings, plasma packs and ampoules of morphine. "Yes, of course, it's in the cupboard, bottom shelf," he pointed to the storage cupboards on the other side of the room. Lenya went over and retrieved the heavy bag and as she turned, Andy rose to his feet. "I'll make this easier, I'll go to the bathroom and wash my hands and face then get out of these clothes." *Well, what's left of them anyway!*

"Okay."

Andy headed to the bathroom, before he closed the door he saw Lenya opening the medical pack. He turned the hot tap on and let the water run for a minute while the hot water came through the pipes. Andy touched the water to test its warmth. *That will do.* He placed the plug in the sink allowing the water to pool. When the sink was three-quarters full, he turned the tap off and splashed the hot water onto his face.

Then he lent forward and immersed his face into the pool of water, splashing the water over his hair and behind his neck and ears. The warm water stung as it washed over his cuts. He carefully rubbed his skin and scalp to remove the dirt and grime which had stuck to him. Andy straightened up and grabbed a large towel to gently dry his head, face and neck.
Looking in the mirror, he gave himself a tired smile as he thought about his good fortune at not being badly injured in the explosion. Before he could place his hands in the now dirty, blood stained water, he heard a sound which made him freeze on the spot. He listened. He wanted to be certain on what he was hearing. The distinctive sound from the throbbing engine of a large motorcycle ... a very familiar motorcycle. The noise stopped.

Andy opened the door from the bathroom and quickly headed for the television screen which showed the live feeds from the cameras.

"What's up?" Lenya asked.

"I just need to look at something," he replied with a growing unease. His instincts were right as he looked at the feeds. Several armed men were entering the building from the main street and more making their way up the fire escape. *Shit! How the hell did you find me here?* Andy headed for the gun-safe and quickly keyed in the combination. The door opened and he reached for the hand grenades, which he put into the pockets of Winchester's leather jacket, and the flash bangs, which he stuffed down the front of the jacket.

"What are you doing?" Lenya sounded concerned.

"I think something bad is going to happen and I just want to be ready." He reached in the safe for the AR15 and grabbed the two full, extended magazines which he placed into his trouser pockets. He looked at the Glock, then turned to Lenya. "Do you shoot?" her horrified expression told him the answer.

"No. Why would I? You're starting to scare me."

He left the Glock in the open safe and returned to the screen. There were five men preparing to enter via the fire escape and, at the door of his apartment, six men were lined-up, their weapons at the ready. The camera feed from the front of the building showed more armed men entering the building and the man with the motorcycle directing the activity. He turned to Lenya and said, "Lenya, you need to trust me, I need you to go into the bathroom and lock the door."

She didn't move. He could see she was terrified … terrified of … him. Then Lenya made an unexpected move; she ran away from him and towards the apartment door. "Nooooo!" he screamed, but it was too late and before Lenya's hand reached for the door handle, the wood splintered, her body jerked and spun as several bullets ripped through her. The sound of the automatic gunfire was deafening. Lenya's body was cruelly tossed around in some weird, jerky dance before it fell to the ground in a contorted heap of blood and gore.

Andy felt a surge of pure rage flow through him. Without a pause he flicked up the safety covers of the Claymores and threw both metal switches. The building shook from the simultaneous explosions. Andy ran forwards, he didn't have time to dwell on Lenya's dead body, as he made towards the door. He opened it, but remained inside the apartment.

Andy reached inside his jacket for a flash bang. He held the device in his right hand, firmly gripped the safety lever and pulled the pin with his left index finger. He tossed it through the doorway into the corridor and seconds later the deafening explosion and resulting percussion gave Andy the opportunity he needed to sprint from the apartment. He saw five men lying in the corridor bleeding out from the Claymore. Further along, two more armed men were standing but looked disorientated, he squeezed off two rounds into each of them as he continued to run down the corridor to the door for the stairwell.

He hit the fire alarm on the wall, immediately immobilizing the lifts. His plan to force those assaulting him onto the stairs. Then he reached into his trouser pocket for a grenade. Despite the commotion in the corridor, no residents had started to leave their apartments. He hoped that meant they were either at work or too afraid to open their doors, so, as he reached the stairwell door, he took a calculated risk; grasping the grenade, he pulled its pin, opened a door and tossed it through the gap. A burst of machine gun fire tore through the door as it closed. Seconds later the grenade detonated, the concrete stairwell amplifying its percussion.

Andy took a deep breath, opened the door to the stairwell, and entered the space. Two armed men lay motionless on the floor, another at the top of the stairs rested on his knees in shock at the surprise counter attack. Two more attackers were looking up somewhat dazed from the level below. Andy pointed his rifle at the two men on the lower level: first, the one on the left took two rounds to the chest; he switched his aim to the man to the second, his eyes reflected fear, before two rounds tore through his chest and he dropped. Finally, Andy took out the man on his knees at the top of the stairs with a burst on automatic. The body was knocked backwards and tumbled to join his colleagues in a neat pile at the bottom of the stairs.

The sound of the fire alarm, explosions and shooting had now drawn cautious residents from their apartments. The stairwell started to fill. He knew if he pursued other armed men, there could be many civilian casualties. As he made his way back to his apartment, residents spilled into the corridor, their faces couldn't hide their look of shock and disgust at the sight of the dead men with their twisted and bloodied bodies. Andy didn't make eye contact with his neighbors, instead he focused on any imminent threats. He pushed his bullet riddled apartment door open and closed it behind him.

He stopped when he saw Lenya's blood covered body. Her dull, lifeless eyes stared into the distance; the spark of life extinguished from them. He felt a pang of painful emotion tear into him; despite himself he had become involved with this beautiful woman. They'd warned them about emotional attachments at The Farm but he couldn't resist her charm and naturally, he thought he would be immune to feelings. He fought back the natural urge to stay with her. *Sorry Lenya. This was never meant to happen.*

Above the sound of the fire alarm, Andy heard the distinctive, now familiar, guttural sound of the motorcycle roar away; its rider satisfied that Andy wasn't likely to walk away from the assault. The noise brought Andy back to the present. He moved to the gun safe where he placed the AR-15 in its rack, removed the magazines from his pockets and put them on a shelf in the safe. He added two tear gas grenades together with the other ordinance on the inside of the leather jacket. He pocketed the glock magazines before picking up the pistol and placing it in his jacket pocket.

With all of the firepower he wanted, Andy closed and locked the gun safe before he opened his document safe and removed his passports together with an envelope of cash. He locked the document safe and, before abandoning the apartment for good, snatched his grab bag. He headed into his bedroom, opened the window and climbed onto the ancient fire escape, which protested under his weight as he stepped on to it. He made his way down, passing the shredded bodies of the former attackers and soon he was joining the line of residents also brave enough to use the aging structure to escape to the ground.

He stepped off the last rung and mingled with the other residents, using the opportunity to take in the scene, blend in with the crowd and stay invisible in the aftermath of the assault on the building. The sirens from approaching emergency vehicles grew louder. Onlookers were quickly gathering to see what had happened, though only a small number offered help to the elderly or those overwhelmed by the terrible scene. Andy slowly made his way to the edge of the onlookers, and, with a plan forming in his mind, he finally slipped clear and headed back to the leveled field office building he'd left less than thirty minutes earlier.

Approaching the smoldering site, he saw something lying above the rubble on the periphery, the image of a painted dragon on a shiny black object. No one stopped him as he reached through the tape and grabbed the motorcycle helmet. With a confident stride he approached Winchester's sports bike and attached his pack to the rear of the motorbike. He donned the helmet, climbed onto the machine, kicked off its stand and fired up the bikes powerful engine. Seconds later he effortlessly guided the motorcycle through the streets and out of the city.

CHAPTER 11

Once outside the city, Andy opened the throttle and pushed the bike to its limits making the road markings streak past in a blur. The straight road had little traffic making it easy to cruise in the outside lane as he headed towards Kiev. In the back of his mind he knew he had to call Langley, but not while he made such good progress. Riding hard and with Luhansk four hours behind him, fatigue started to creep up; he'd been through one hell of a day. The fuel gauge showed just under half a tank when a highway sign indicated a gas stop ten kilometers ahead.

I'll fill the tank, stretch my legs and phone Langley. Then press on.

Three minutes later, Andy slowed the bike to take the exit. The fuel stop had six gas pumps and a single story building with a cash teller, shop and toilets. Next to the building he noticed a rest area with four wooden benches. At one of the benches six, well-built, military-age men, were talking amongst themselves. Andy pulled up at a gas pump and glanced again at the men. Next to them were parked two cars.

He recognized the red rear window sticker and the distinctive scratch on the bumper. *That's Stalinki's Audi.* He could feel a burning rage rising within him and his fatigue evaporated … the men who had killed Lenya and his co-workers were sat right in front of him. Andy kept his helmet on while he fueled the motorcycle before he headed inside to pay. Approaching the cashier Andy removed his helmet and paid for his fuel.

Two men dressed in denim trousers, black tee-shirts and black leather jackets had been loitering near the confectionery, they'd grabbed handfuls of snacks and queued behind Andy. He paid for his fuel and headed to the public pay phone in the corner when he noticed both men wore Russian army combat boots. *Are these two guys part of the team at the bench?* Andy couldn't be certain, but it was more likely than not. He didn't think they would be looking for him as, by his timings, they would have had to be clear of Luhansk before the firefight at his apartment.

He fed the pay phone a fist full of coins and dialed the Ukrainian access number for Langley's crisis management center. The call was answered in four rings.

"Hello. Welcome to Global Exports service desk. Your call is important to us. To help with the routing of your call, please select from one of the following options. Please press one for sales. Press two for an existing account enquiry. Three for support."

Andy knew that making one of these selections would put him into voicemail which no one listened to. The next prompt was the one he needed. "If you know the extension of the person you wish to speak with, please enter their extension number followed by the hash key." Andy keyed in the emergency code *219931#*. "Please stay on the line while we direct your call."

He heard a click, then a female voice: "Good morning. Please authenticate yourself?

"Flint. 24825062. Black."

"Please hold the line." The line went quiet for a moment, then, "Mr. Flint, this line is not secure. Can you confirm your location?"

"I'm on my way to Kiev from Luhansk, I'm over half-way and calling from a gas stop."

"Mr. Flint please hold while I connect you to the duty officer."

Andy heard a click before a deep male voice came onto the line: "Mr. Flint, I'm here to help, before we get going I've got to remind you this line is not secure."

"Copy that."

"We have lost communication with our station in Luhansk, we've received reports indicating an incident of some kind, can you confirm?"

"Yes. The building was leveled in an explosion." Andy looked out through the window at the group of men and watched as one of them, the apparent leader, received a cell phone call.

"What is the status of the other agents?"

"All dead."

"Can you confirm?"

"Yes. All dead." Andy continued to watch the man outside as he answered the call. The man looked in Andy's direction, their eyes briefly met.

"Protocol states you should stay at the safe house until assistance arrives. Andy, can you explain why you didn't follow protocol?"

"My safe house came under attack. They killed my girlfriend. I had to abandon the location as it was no longer ... er, safe. That's why I didn't follow protocol and, now, I'm en-route to Kiev where I can reach safety and report in."

"Andy, you are instructed to return to the field station; we'll extract you there as per standard protocol."

Andy scratched his head. *Go back to Luhansk? ... you have got to be kidding me!* Andy looked outside, he saw the man with the phone directing the others around him ... and now they all carried pistols. *Shit!*
"Gotta go," Andy said into the receiver and hung up. He headed for the restrooms and closed the door as two of the men ran into the building through the main entrance. Andy didn't believe they'd seen him enter the female restroom. He noticed in the rest room there were high windows, but not too high to prevent him from climbing out. He placed the helmet on the closed lid of the toilet seat and removed a tear-gas grenade from inside his leather jacket before making his way back to the entrance door for the restroom.

Andy gripped the tear-gas grenade in his right hand and pulled the pin. Opening the door just a few inches he tossed the grenade into the room and quickly closed it. Turning and moving quickly, he grabbed the helmet from the seat just as he heard a loud pop; the tear-gas grenade had detonated and he could hear people coughing. He stood on the toilet seat, reached up and climbed through the open window.

Crouched with his back to the building, Andy gripped the glock and chambered a round. *This helmet isn't helping. I can't carry it. I need both hands to fight.* He briefly thought about leaving the helmet, but retrieving it afterwards would slow him down and, after his previous contact with these guys, he knew he needed to get clear of the area ... and fast. He put the helmet on and pushed the visor up. His vision forward was clear but his hearing was now muffled.

He reached inside his jacket for a flash-bang and, holding it with his left hand, pulled the pin to arm it with his right. He edged to the corner of the building and slowly peered around the length which led towards the forecourt … his way was clear. With the pistol in his right hand pointing ahead and the primed flash-bang in his left, Andy quickly advanced along the side of the building.

He paused briefly before the next corner, allowing himself a few seconds to recall the layout of the station: to the front an open forecourt; to his immediate left the entrance to the shop; and, on the far side of the building, the two cars and benches where the men had been sitting. *I've got to move.* He turned the corner with the pistol pointing straight ahead, ready for whatever situation he'd face.

Two men stood in the center of the forecourt, pistols raised and ready to fire, their focus on the doorway. By the time the first one had seen Andy, Andy had put one round into his chest; a fraction of a second later, the second man was felled by two rounds to the chest. With a left-handed throw, Andy lobbed the flash-bang towards the cars where two of the armed men had taken cover.

The flash-bang glanced off the building and spun through the air. The two men, who had already seen their buddies fall, watched the spinning grenade as it arced through the air towards them. They had just enough time to duck behind a car before it landed and detonated … six-feet in front of the blue Audi. Andy put the glock down and reached inside his jacket for the second flash-bang.

Without a pause he squeezed the grenade's handle and pulled the pin. Holding the flash-bang with his arm extended out as far as possible, he tossed the flash-bang high into the air aiming for it to detonate behind the second car. Andy didn't wait to see where it landed. He retrieved his pistol form the floor, "Best defense is offense!" he told himself as he sprinted towards the two cars.

Time appeared to slow down as he closed in on the two cars and the armed men taking cover. He could see their heads start to rise up and he knew that they would see him running towards them and open fire. Andy raised the pistol as he ran, aiming where he expected the men would appear. He saw the flash-bang disappear behind the car and detonate close to the two men with a blinding flash and loud explosion.

Andy continued running towards his target as both men appeared with their hands over ears and staggering unsteadily while dazed by the effect of the flash-bang. Andy stopped less than ten feet from the cars and fired two rounds into the gunman on the right and two rounds into the gunman on the left; both dropped on the spot.

As he was checking whether they were neutralized, the main door of the shop opened and three men still carrying their pistols staggered out. They were rubbing their eyes as the tear gas had blinded them, rubbing them only made the effect worse. *Good, the tear gas has done its job; now it's time I did mine.* Andy put one round into each of them as they took their first and, now possibly, their last breath of fresh air. Andy changed his magazine for a full one.

One more gunman inside along with the cashier. Andy felt conflicted: Go after the eighth gunman or leave and continue to Kiev. With his decision made, Andy took cover behind the second car and removed a hand-grenade from inside his jacket. He primed it, tossed it under the car near the engine, and sprinted towards the cover of the Audi to shelter himself as much as possible from the impending explosion. Moments later the grenade detonated, the car jumped as though it had sneezed.

Andy looked at the main entrance of the building, then quickly glanced towards the rear, in case the last gunman had used the same tactic he had and climbed out of the rear window to out-flank him. All was clear, Andy armed another tear-gas grenade, open the door of the Audi and tossed the grenade into the passenger foot-well, closing the door quickly to allow the tear-gas to fill the enclosed space.

Turning, he ran past the second car which now bled a mixture of oil and water over the forecourt. Even with his helmet on he heard the pop of the tear-gas grenade ... *That car ain't going nowhere without being decontaminated*! He reached Winchester's Kawasaki, mounted it and fired up the engine. Kicking the motorcycle off its stand and keeping low against the machines large gas tank he twisted the throttle and accelerated away on the open road towards Kiev.

CHAPTER 12

Andy felt tired after the days' events, but he still had to find a safe haven. His adrenaline high had long gone and, in addition to the cuts and bruises from the explosion, his body ached from the effort of controlling the sports bike at speed. A wave of relief washed over him as he pulled up outside the guardroom of the US Embassy on Aviakonstructor Igor Sikorsky Street. He dismounted, removed his helmet and approached the guardroom window, with its thick ballistic glass, behind which sat two marines in full dress uniform.

"How can we help, sir?" one of the marines asked Andy.

"I'm a US Government agent from Luhansk and I need to see Jamie Ross from the Trade and Culture Department."

"Do you have an appointment, sir?"

"No, but she will see me" he replied.

The second marine picked up the phone and made a call.

"Can I see some ID please, sir?" the first marine asked. Andy slid his US passport through the narrow slot under the glass. "May I see your government ID please, sir?" he asked.

"In my line of work, I don't carry a government ID!" Andy failed to hide the irritation in his voice. He watched as the second marine slowly thumbed through his passport while speaking on the phone; he assumed the marine had Ross on the line. The marine hung up, stood, placed Andy's passport on a glass plate and took a scan before scooping it up and sliding it back to him through the narrow slot.

"Sir, please come through this door." the second marine pointed to the pedestrian access door.

"Can I bring my bike inside the compound?" he asked as he turned to face the sports bike.

"No. You must leave it outside. No one will touch it while it's parked right there." the marine replied.

"Are you sure?"

The first marine pressed a button and the pedestrian door emitted a loud buzz as the lock released. Andy held his hand up, "Hang on a minute." Andy went back to the bike. He opened his grab bag and placed the glock, magazines and remaining flashbang grenade inside the bag before zipping it back up and making sure it was secure again. Andy presented himself at the door as the, now worried-looking, marine watched him enter the guardhouse.

"Sir, should you be leaving your pistol in a bag out on the street?" the marine asked.

Andy shrugged his shoulders. "Like you said, no one will touch it."

The first marine approached Andy with an electronic wand, "Sir, please spread your arms out?"
Andy made a star shape as he spread his arms out and parted his legs. The marine slowly passed the wand around Andy's body, it gave a high pitched electronic screech as it went over Andy's belt buckle. The marine paused and looked at Andy's belt. Andy removed his belt and handed it to the marine who carefully examined it with an unexpected thoroughness. *Next he'll want me to take my shoes off and maybe drop my pants!* Satisfied the belt didn't pose a threat, the marine returned it.

A bespectacled, slightly overweight, middle aged woman wearing a black below the knee dress, white blouse and charcoal gray jacket walked in while Andy threaded his belt through the loops on his pants. The first marine looked at her and pointed to Andy. *This must be Ross and she doesn't look too pleased to see me.*

"Andrew Flint?" the tone of her voice confirmed his assumption.

"Yes. That's me. All the way from Luhansk." Andy gave a tired smile and offered his hand in greeting. Ross didn't respond, instead she remained no closer than three feet away from him as though he carried a contagious infection. She briefly looked him up and down.

"We weren't expecting you, come with me," Andy started to follow, "you can leave the helmet with them." Andy placed the helmet on one of the two large desks and followed Ross out of the guardroom into the main compound walking briskly towards the Embassy building. The large, imposing concrete building looked to have been constructed in the sixties. Ross appeared to have read his mind as she spoke. "This was the former Communist Party headquarters. When they were kicked out. We moved in. After the Presidential Palace, this is the best building in the country."

"Were you here when that happened?" Andy asked as a way to build rapport.

"No. I've been here for just over a year. I'd been working in Britain. Everything was sweet. Then one day, right out of the blue I get posted here. They told me it was temporary, six months' tops." She stopped and turned to look at Andy. "Here I am a year later and they claim they never said it was temporary. My husband stayed in the UK, he didn't want to move here." Ross's expression changed, she looked sad. "Last week my husband wrote and has asked for a divorce." *Jeez, I wasn't expecting your life story lady, just breaking the ice between us!*

Ross used both arms to pull hard at the tall, solid wooden main entrance door to open it. Inside they were met by two more uniformed marines, both wearing side-arms. "He's with me." Ross announced as she walked passed them and through another heavy door into a red carpeted corridor. She led Andy to a windowless meeting room which had a cheap wooden table and four leather office chairs set on wheels. "Come in. Sit down. May I get you anything?"

"Black coffee." Andy replied. He didn't follow her instruction to sit.

"Okay I'll grab a coffee for you. By the way, have you eaten?"

Andy realized he'd not eaten since breakfast and he could feel his energy levels quickly dropping. "Not since last night." Ross headed for the door.

"I'll grab you a coffee and see what's available from the cafeteria."

"Thanks, I'd appreciate some food."

Ross left Andy alone. After pacing for a few minutes he sat in the chair closest to the door. He thought about Ross and how the agency had helped end her marriage. His thoughts were disturbed by a loud thumping against the door. Andy stood and opened the door to Ross. In her hands she carried a gray plastic tray upon which were two coffees' in paper takeaway cups and an aluminum thermal plate cover. She placed the tray on the table and removed the cover to reveal a white plate with a burger set in a bun and to the side a stack of fries. Andy's mouth salivated as the smell of the fatty food hit him. Ross grabbed her coffee and sat facing Andy.
"Tuck in, before it goes cold."

"Thank you." Andy sat and grabbed a handful of fries which he shoveled into his mouth.

"What happened in Luhansk?" she asked.

"My assets were murdered," he said between mouthfuls.

"The Schwartz's and Mikhail Stalinki?" Ross asked.

"Yes, they were executed." Andy took a sip of the coffee.

"Executed? That's a big call. How can you be certain?"

"When I heard of Stalinki's death I crossed the border and went to see his body at the morgue."

Ross looked horrified. "Did you get clearance to cross the border? Do you know how many rules you've broken? Do you know how big a diplomatic incident you could have caused? God this is a mess!"

Andy held up his hand, interrupting Ross. "Please let me finish." Ross stopped and nodded for Andy to continue. "No one cleared it. After the murder of the station chief the guys should have been allowed to carry arms. Even after the murder of the Schwartz's, the order to carry arms still didn't come through. Why not?"

"Langley wouldn't authorize it."

"We were sure someone in the chain was leaking information. I read Stalinski's file. He wanted to get his green card and he was helping us as a way to get support for his application. Whoever put a bullet in the back of his head, also put a single piece of green card in his pocket."

"What?"

"That's right. His killer knew about his aim to secure a green card. How?" Andy let the question hang in the air as he took a large bite of the double patty burger.

"There could have been a leak from the Luhansk station? Ross suggested.

"Okay. There's this guy on a motorcycle. I saw him at the border on both occasions when our assets crossed. He followed them.

Just before the station was bombed and I was buried in the rubble, I heard the same motorcycle. After my apartment was attacked, I heard the same motorcycle again. Tell me that was just a coincidence?"

"You can't be certain it was him. The report we've received from the Ukrainians said the station's destruction was due to a gas explosion from the restaurant below."

"Do you really believe that? The whole building was leveled. I was lucky to survive, the other three ... not so fortunate." Ross shook her head in disbelief. "The guys at the station believed Danny Lynch had been murdered. Lynch was fit and into martial arts. The idea that some street punk took him out with a few lucky punches and then shot him, doesn't work for me, especially as they left his watch, wallet and car keys. Following Lynch's murder, we've seen more murders and an increase in Russian military activity. All a big coincidence? What do you think?" Andy paused to allow his words to sink in and took another healthy bite from his burger while he waited for Ross to respond.

"The conclusion around the reason for Lynch's murder came from Langley after they'd reviewed all of the data and evidence. They're the experts. Plus, there could have been a leak at the field station."

Andy finished his mouthful of burger, "So explain this ... all the guys in the office are dead. I'm on my way to Kiev and stop to fill up with gas. I check in with Langley and, while I'm talking some thug outside receives a call on his cell and he looks straight at me. Moments later they're coming for me ... now tell me, who called them from beyond the grave, Winchester, Kowalski or Yevenko?"

Ross was still for several seconds as she stared at Andy, then reached for her coffee and slowly took a sip. Not to be the one to break the awkward silence between them, Andy ate more fries and took another bite from his burger while watching Ross. She broke first.

"Look, I'm going to share my personal opinion, okay? Not the official BS from Langley, I believe something is wrong and, either Langley can't see it, or they don't want to see it."

"So you believe me?

Ross nodded and took a sip of her coffee before she spoke, "Your photograph … the one of the man on the motorcycle?"

"Yes?" Andy leaned forward with interest.

"The face belongs to John Crofton." Andy's expression remained blank, the name meant nothing to him.

CHAPTER 13

"Who the hell is John Crofton?" Andy asked.

"I don't know much as his file is sealed. He's been dead for two years … he was a highly regarded agency field agent."

"Come on," Andy protested. "You must know more."

"All I know is Crofton was a member of the black ops team. Crofton undertook our black bag operations."

"Black bag?"

"When the agency needed someone killed or permanently disappeared. That's when they call upon a specialist with … particular skills."

"An agency hit man?"

Ross nodded, "His file said he was killed in a climbing accident in the Himalayas. It said an avalanche took him while making a solo ascent of Everest. That was two years ago and then, you posted your photograph. I used the agency's facial recognition system and the search spat out Crofton's details, however, when I passed the information up the chain of command, Langley overrode it … said it wasn't him."

"Why do you think they'd do that?" Andy took another sip of his strong coffee which had cooled down slightly so it didn't burn his tongue, and it was good.

"Lies and deception are our bread and butter. You know that … it's what we do. You shouldn't be surprised to find there's another game in play."

"What is the other game?" Andy scratched his head. "Why would a dead agency black ops specialist who you identified as John Crofton be in Luhansk?" Ross remained silent as Andy continued, "We know covert Russian military and intelligence agents are operating inside the Ukraine. Is Crofton involved with the Russian military buildup? What do you know?"

Ross closed her mouth and briefly pursed her lips. "From satellite imagery and intercepted radio chatter, the build-up has continued. I believe an invasion of the Ukraine is imminent. The Russian Government denies any knowledge of a build-up. The confirmation by your assets would have helped complete our picture. Langley knows all of this but appears to be doing nothing."

"What do the Ukrainian Government think of the Russian activity?" he asked.
"They're terrified. They don't want to mobilize their forces because this could enrage the Russians and create a situation where the Russians view their mobilization as a provocative act and use it for the pretext to invade. The Ukrainians also know that if they don't mobilize there's no way they could even slow the Russians from reaching their Western border with Poland. The Ukrainian Government is seeking Western support. They want us to help them. ... but we're not."

Andy lent back and rubbed the stubble on his chin while he thought about the situation. "I think Crofton is somehow tied up in all of this. He's deliberately blunted our ability to see what's happening on the ground. But worse, Langley don't think Crofton is alive and probably won't sanction any resources to find him."

"I agree and Langley won't waste precious resources searching for a dead man." Andy grabbed a few of the now cold fries and chewed on them, the salt making him thirsty.

"Do you want to help find Crofton?" he stared into Ross's brown eyes and held her gaze before he continued, "I have an idea."

Ross sat up. "Yes. I want to help, but if they won't allow us to search for him, how will we find him?"

"Can you have the satellite image recognition software track the motorcycle Crofton is using. I believe he rode it to the field station bombing and again when they attacked my apartment murdering my girlfriend. That gives two reference points from today ... and, maybe, a third if you go back to the day Lynch was murdered."

"It is possible, but how do we keep it under Langley's radar?"

"Remember we aren't tracking Crofton ... we will be tracking a motorcycle which a person of interest could have been using at the time."

Ross paused for a moment. "Then, yes, I can help. Let me go upstairs and make some inquiries." Andy stood as if to join her. "Where do you think you're going? Sit down." Andy froze for a moment, confused. *I thought we were a team on this.* "The agency ordered you back to Luhansk so that's where they believe you're heading. If you come upstairs with me, within minutes, Langley will know you're here. From what you've said, maybe someone at Langley is helping Crofton."

Andy sat.

"Do you need anything else?"

After eating the fatty food and sitting in a warm room, Andy felt fatigue creeping up. "Just some rest." he covered his mouth as he tried to stifle a yawn.
"I sometimes sleep here, so I have a cot and a sleeping bag upstairs. If you don't mind using them, I can bring them down here for you. I'll book this room out so you're not disturbed."

"Thanks. That's very kind of you." Ross left the room, leaving Andy to finish the last of his cold burger.

***

He heard the door open and the flick of the light switch, then a female voice, "Andy wake up."

Andy opened his eyes to see Ross looking down at him. She placed a mug of steaming coffee onto the table. He looked at his watch, ten past seven in the morning. Andy rubbed his eyes, then looked at the coffee. "Thanks, I'm going to need this today!"

"Did you sleep?"

"Like a baby!" he knew she hadn't woken him just to ask him how he slept, "What's the latest?"

Ross smiled, an excited look spread across her face, "Your idea worked. We were able to find the motorcycle and, with our extensive satellite coverage, we've been able to track its movement. More importantly we didn't set off any red flags at Langley."

Andy unzipped the warm sleeping bag, climbed out still fully dressed and started putting on his shoes, "What else did you find?"

"Firstly, you were right. The motorcycle had been at both the destruction of the Luhansk field station and the attack on your apartment."

"Where did it go after that?"

"This is where it gets interesting, the software tracked it all the way to the Russian naval base at Sevastopol on the Black Sea."

"When did he get there?"

"Less than an hour ago."

"Something important must be happening. I'd like to go there and find out."

"What? You've been attacked and almost killed twice in the last twenty-four hours! You know you are a marked man? Going back isn't a good idea ... bloody stupid actually!"

"Crofton is involved in this ... and so are the Russians."

"It will take hours to get you there."

"What about the Ambassadors jet?"

"Are you serious? The moment I ask for use of that jet, Langley will be informed and, if you want to stay 'under the radar', it isn't an option."

Andy scratched his head while he thought about the situation, "Are you in communications with the Ukrainian Government?"

"Yes, they're worried about the Russian build up and also the Russian covert intelligence activities."

"Could you arrange for the Ukrainian Government to get me to the base in Sevastopol?" he watched her eyes light up. *This is probably the most excitement she's had in years.*

"I'll ask. I can't promise anything I can't ask that question over the phone for obvious reasons. I'll have to go across town... Before I head out, I'll bring you some breakfast and a towel along with some toiletries so you can freshen up while I'm gone."

"Thanks." *It would be even better if you could get me a fresh set of clothes that don't look like I've slept in them.* Ross smiled at Andy and left him. While he was alone Andy rolled up the sleeping bag and dismantled the cot, placing it back into its carrying bag.

Ross returned carrying a tray which she carefully placed on the table. She removed a cream colored towel which she'd had draped over her shoulder, throwing it to Andy which he caught with his left hand. Andy removed the plate cover to reveal a full cooked breakfast complete with hash browns and fried eggs.

"This is great. Thank you."

"You're welcome." Andy put the towel down and sat at the table, reaching for the cutlery. Ross spoke while Andy started cutting into the pork sausages. "I've spoken with my Ukrainian counterpart; I'm meeting him for a coffee in twenty minutes. Let's see what he can do to help. By the way did you find the restrooms last night?"

Andy smiled. "Do you see that wet patch in the corner?" He pointed with his fork. The smile on Ross's face vanished and was replaced with a look of horror as she turned towards the corner where Andy had indicated. He burst out laughing. "Sure I found them, out of the door and to the right, complete with showers and changing room." Her smile returned, this time with an edge of nervousness about it, then she headed for the door. "If we are going to work together you'll get used to my sense of humor!"

"I'll see you later." Andy didn't have time to reply before she'd gone so he got on with finishing his breakfast and downing the strong black coffee. *This is good!*

CHAPTER 14

By the time Ross returned, Andy had showered, and, though he would have liked a fresh set of clothes, it was good to be clean and well-fed. … and a, seemingly, endless supply of good strong black coffee. "How was your meeting?"

"It couldn't have gone any better, I gave him information on what happened in Luhansk and in return he agreed to get you to Sevastopol the quickest way possible. While I was with him he made some calls and it's all arranged."

"As easy as that?"

"Yes!" Ross sounded annoyed. "What we've done is tip the Ukrainian Government off that something is going down in Sevastopol. They knew about the Russian build up near Miller-ovo and now they'll move their forces to the Crimea to protect their key points and critical infrastructure should the Russians launch an offensive from the base. I'd say it's a fair trade when the very survival of their country is at stake."

"When you put it that way. When can I leave?"

"Shortly, I want to give you a laser microphone which integrates with the satellite phone you're taking. If you do learn something, then Langley can hear about it in real time too."

"Okay. *"I'm impressed, she's achieved the near impossible in a very short space of time, but I'm not quite ready to let my defenses down; I've lost too many people recently.*

"I'll be back with your gear, and then I'll tell you where to catch your ride." Ross headed out and was gone for nearly ten minutes. She returned carrying a canvas bag which she placed on the table, unzipped and opened it for Andy to see what lay inside. "Binoculars, laser microphone and satellite comms with an extra two fully charged batteries. The batteries add a bit of weight, but I think the extra transmission time will be worth the inconvenience for you. To activate the satellite comms you'll need to enter the access code 8Z1T2U#"

Andy put on Winchester's leather motorcycle jacket and zipped up the holdall. "Where do I need to get to?"

"Boryspil Air Base. It borders onto the international airport. It's eighteen miles east of here so you can get there in less than half an hour on your bike. When you arrive at the guard room ask for Colonel Andrej Andrudski. He'll take care of things from there."

"Thanks." Andy picked up the holdall and made for the door with Ross following close behind. Andy continued to lead until he reached the main entrance door and pressed the door release. He opened the door wide for Ross to step through, and then he followed her into the courtyard. As they approached the guard room, the door opened and out stepped a tall marine in dress uniform who held the door open for the two of them. Ross walked inside and headed straight for the exit door. Andy grabbed the helmet he'd left with the guards the previous evening and followed Ross outside.

The motorcycle looked untouched. He quickly looked in the bag which he'd left with the motorcycle. The pistol, loaded magazines and stun grenade were still there. He closed the bag and put the holdall which Ross had given him onto his back and climbed onto the Kawasaki. "I'll call you from the naval base." Andy slipped on the helmet, inserted the key into the ignition and pressed the start button. The powerful engine fired up, when Andy briefly twisted the throttle its engine roared.

"Good luck." Ross called out over the noise.

Andy kicked the bike off its stand and after a quick look over his shoulder pulled away onto the road, seconds later he'd turned onto the main highway. The roar of the racing bikes engine carried to Ross long after Andy had left her sight. The signs for the air base were easy for Andy to pick out which helped account for his arrival at the guard room of the air base in just under fifteen minutes. Four soldiers dressed in full combat gear nervously handled their rifles as the senior non-commissioned officer left the warmth of the small brick guard room and approached him.

"How can we help you today? The sergeant asked. Andy noticed that unlike the four soldiers stood outside, the sergeant wasn't wearing body armor or a Kevlar helmet and, instead of a 7.62 semi-automatic rifle, he wore a pistol on his right hip.

Rank certainly does have its privileges .. except in a fire fight of course! "I have a meeting with Colonel Andrej Andrudski." The sergeant briefly nodded. "Stay here." The sergeant re-entered the guard room and, moments later, reappeared accompanied by a second man dressed in a dark blue suit with a dark shirt which was brought to life with a bright pop of color from his light yellow tie. "I'm Andrej Andrudski and you are?"

"Andy Flint. Jamie Ross sent me." The colonel nodded and offered Andy his hand to shake.

"My car is over there" he pointed to a battered yellow Fiat parked behind the barrier in the area marked for visitor parking. "Follow me while I drive. Everybody is a little nervous, so please stay close to me. If we get separated, stop and I will come back for you." Andrudski headed towards his car as the sergeant barked his orders. Two soldiers ran from the guard room, they wore body armor, had their rifles slung across their chests and wore berets, not helmets. One of them headed for the barrier, the other stood next to his buddy and waved Andy on as the white barrier arm was raised, clearing Andy's way ahead.

Andy rode slowly towards Andrudski and caught up with him by the time he entered his car. The Fiat didn't sound reliable as it took the engine three attempts to start with Andrudski turning the key and pumping the gas each time. When it finally started, Andy watched the Fiat emit a large plume of black oily smoke out of the exhaust. Andrudski pulled forward and raised his left hand giving Andy a thumbs up signal.

Andrudski is clearly pleased his car actually started this time, Andy thought. He followed closely behind the Fiat, sucking in the cars toxic fumes as they slowly worked their way through the base. Andrudski led them close to the runway and to a single story wooden building which had a rusty tin roof. The structure looked as if it had seen better times and, like Andrudski's car, was in need of some basic maintenance. Andy couldn't be sure if Andrudski had stopped the car when he parked or the car had stalled. Either way, he hadn't parked within a marked bay and it looked like he had no intention of trying to move the car into a better parked position as he climbed out, locked the door and stepped back, briefly examining his appalling parking.

Andy rode the motorcycle into the middle of the space next to Andrudski and stopped the engine with a single button push. With the bike pulled onto its stand, Andy pocketed the key and removed the holdall and his grab bag from the rear of the bike. Now the memory came back to Andy that in addition to food, the grab bag contained water, a medical pack and some cash, a toothbrush, toothpaste and a cheap razor. "You'll not be able to take all of that with you." Andrudski said as he pointed to the bag on Andy's back and the other held in his right hand.

Andy held up the one in his hand. "This is just so I can freshen up. I'll leave it with you if that's okay?" He followed the colonel into the building and was surprised by its modern and clean interior. They'd stepped into a common room, complete with casual seating, a pool table and a large television streaming German MTV. Andrudski led Andy through the common room to a briefing room where aviation maps covered one wall. On a large table positioned in the middle of the room was a Perspex covered map of the Ukraine. Andy could see colored lines which pilots had previously drawn onto the Perspex as part of their route planning.

"Please sit." Andrudski gestured to one of the orange plastic chairs which surrounded the table. Andy sat as instructed. "It is good to meet you Andy." Andrudski looked briefly at his watch, then continued. "You arrived early. Your pilot will not be here for another ten minutes. Why don't you quickly freshen up in the bathroom and then I'll brief you. But please be quick, there will not be much time when your pilot arrives."

"Great. Where do I need to go?"

Andrudski pointed to the left. "Over there. Second door on the right."

"Thanks." Andy stood and took both bags with him to the bathroom. Inside, Andy opened the grab bag and reached for the clear plastic package which contained toiletries which he ripped open. He took the toothbrush, briefly ran the cold tap and rinsed his new toothbrush in the cold water. It was then Andy saw the sink only had the one tap which only ran cold. *Damn, it's going to be a cold water shave.*
Brushing his teeth, he enjoyed the refreshing taste of mint from the paste. The brush quickly removed the furry coating which had formed on his teeth. Rinsing his mouth with cold water revived him. Instead of shaving in cold water, Andy decided to save time and prevent himself from slashing his face with the cheap razor, he'd just wash his face. He reached for the bar of soap, removed it from its packaging and tried to generate lather with the cold water. *Not great, but it will do.*

The cold water helped to wake him up and sharpen his mind. Andy washed the soap from his hands, then cupped them to collect the water which he used to rinse his face and neck. The water started to run down his chin and inside the jacket. Andy reached into the grab bag for a small, quick drying towel which he used to mop the water from his chin. He unzipped his jacket and wiped where the water had dribbled. Now cleaner and somewhat refreshed Andy threw the towel into the grab bag then bent over and rummaged within it.

Got it. He removed a bulky envelope wrapped in clear plastic which he tore away and opened the envelope to reveal a stack of crisp one hundred dollar bills which he pocketed. Replacing the empty envelope and the torn plastic back into the grab bag. Andy picked up both bags and headed back into the common room.

"Feeling better?" Andrudski asked.

"Much." Andy put the bag from Ross on the floor and held up the grab bag. "Can you keep this until I return?"

"Sure."

Andy reached into his trousers for the keys to the motorcycle, then held them up for Andrudski to see. "Can you also look after the bike while I'm away?"

"Sure." Andrudski's smile grew wider.

Andy tossed the keys to him. "Keep it safe."

CHAPTER 15

"Now, let me brief you," Andrudski said, as he unfolded a large map and placed it on the table. Andy moved closer so he had a better view. "I've arranged a flight from here to Kherson Airport." Andrudski lent forward over the table searching for the airport, then he pointed to a spot on the map. "Here." Andy looked at where Andrudski pointed, "A helicopter will fly you to the outskirts of Sevastopol; close enough for you to make your way on foot to the naval base." Andrudski ran his index finger along the map tracing the route from memory. Andy watched closely trying to commit to his memory as much of the terrain as he could.

All of a sudden the colonel stood upright and moved away from the table. "Just wait a moment," he muttered as he walked across to a large, 5-drawer wooden cabinet. He pulled open the top drawer and started searching through papers. "Ah ha!" he shouted in triumph as he turned and held up another chart. Returning to the table, he placed the large scale map onto the table in front of Andy. "This is layout of the naval base."

"I see." *Wow! That's one big base … which is a big advantage as it's bound to have a few vulnerabilities allowing easy access.*

"This is where the helicopter will drop you," Andrudski pointed to the same spot again, "there is a small stream which runs down from the forest above. That will give you enough dead ground to help you avoid detection. The forest is not large, but it does straddle the ridge line from where you'll overlook the base."

Andy looked from one map to the other then nodded his agreement to the route Andrudski was suggesting which, having had the opportunity to look at the maps in front of him, was his preferred option. Andrudski continued, "Make your way down through the trees to the perimeter fence."

"What can you tell me about the fence. Is it guarded? Are there cameras and motion detectors?"

"In this sector," Andrudski pointed to an area on the detailed map they were looking at, "the perimeter fence comprises of metal fencing strips which stand nine feet high with three sharp points at the top; holding onto or putting your bodyweight on the top will not be healthy for you. Once you're over the fence, there is a single track road which follows the fence around the base." Andrudski traced the position of the track around the camp with his finger. "There are regular patrols by armed camp guards who drive the route at least once per hour, even at night."

"What about cameras and sensors?"

"The perimeter of the camp is too big for cameras or motion sensors to be deployed. Inside the main camp there are cameras covering the main entrance, armory, magazine and the wharf areas."

Andy nodded. "You must have done this before. How do I get over the fence?"

Andrudski tried to hide his smile. "In the helicopter I've arranged for a lightweight telescopic ladder for you to take. That will get you over." The two men were interrupted when the main entrance door opened and in strode a man wearing a green flying suit and air force issue sunglasses.

"And here is your pilot right on time." Andrudski announced.

The pilot approached Andy and shook his hand with a firm grip. "Captain Zychan."

"Andy Flint."

"Let's get you kitted out. Colonel, if you'll excuse us." Andrudski nodded to the captain. The captain turned to Andy. "Please come with me," Zychan instructed as he headed out of the common room and down a narrow corridor. Andy picked up the holdall which Ross had given him and followed a few paces behind.

"You can leave the bag here." Andrudski called out. *No chance!* Andy thought as he ignored the request and carried on following the pilot as he entered a small windowless room which had the smell of musty clothing.

"You are slightly taller than me." The pilot rummaged amongst the shelves of green flight suits. "There," he reached for one item and passed it to Andy, "put this on and take that leather jacket off. You'll get too hot in the aircraft." Andy removed his leather jacket and caught a glimpse of Zychan looking at the holdall.

"That's got to go with me." Andy pointed to the holdall. He held up the jacket when he realized it wouldn't fit in the holdall. "Any room for this?"

Zychan shook his head. "No. Your bag alone will be a challenge. The training jet we are using isn't known for comfort or providing space for personal storage." *What the hell have we got. A Ukrainian Air Force crop duster?* Andy climbed into the flying suit as Zychan headed to the other side of the room and selected a green helmet complete with black visor and oxygen mask. As he returned to Andy, Zychan picked a white cotton hat. "Put this on." He handed Andy the cotton hat. Andy did as instructed. Zychan then handed Andy the helmet. "When we get to the aircraft, put the helmet on before you climb the steps to get into the cockpit. The ground crew will be on hand to attach your helmet's hose to the aircraft's oxygen supply."

"Thanks."

"Now there will be lots of instruments and buttons which can be pushed. You'll feel tempted to push some buttons and flick the odd switch, but don't touch anything."

"Okay. I won't." Andy replied defensively feeling like he was being told not to be naughty.

Zychan led Andy out of the fitting room and back into the common room where Andrudski sat and watched them. "Can you keep this for me?" Andy asked Andrudski as he held up the leather jacket.

"Sure" he smiled as he acquired yet more of the American's property.

"You've been briefed?" Zychan asked.

"Yes." Andy replied.

"Great. Let's get you out of here." Zychan announced as he headed for the door and seconds later strode briskly towards a large green aircraft hangar just over a hundred meters away and towards a small side door. Andy struggled to keep up with Zychan as he disappeared through the door just managing to catch the heavy door before it closed. *That would not have looked good … me on the other side and having to knock to enter!*

Inside the hanger, waiting, with metal steps leading to its fully open cockpit canopy, was a Russian built Fulcrum-B fighter-jet. The ground crew were busying themselves as they readied the aircraft for departure.

"Wow!" Andy couldn't disguise his reaction to seeing the aircraft up close.

"Hand your bag over to the ground crew while you climb into the cockpit." Zychan shouted above all the din. Andy realized he couldn't put the helmet on and climb into the aircraft with the holdall in his hands so he reluctantly handed the holdall to a corporal who appeared next to him from nowhere. Andy quickly climbed up the ladder and eased himself into the student's seat as Zychan strapped himself into the pilot's seat. A member of the ground crew connected Zyachan's communications link and oxygen to the aircraft as a second member of the ground crew did the same for Andy. The headset in the helmet made a momentary electronic pop sound, then he could hear Zychan speaking.

"Can you hear me? Just nod or put your thumb up so I know." Zychan voice came through very clear. Andy faced him, nodded and put his left thumb up. The tight webbing-straps made it difficult for Andy to turn and look over his shoulder as the corporal from the ground crew placed Andy's holdall in a small locker built into the fuselage behind the cockpit. "If you need to talk to me, you can either touch the press-to-talk button on your oxygen mask, remember to release when you have finished talking, or press the red button on the top of the control stick."

Andy pressed the small nipple on this oxygen mask and spoke, "I'm really excited about this. I've never flown in a fighter-jet before." He knew there were analysts, intelligence officers and aviation enthusiasts who would give anything just to get a ride in this advanced combat trainer.
"There are sick bags in a pocket to the right of your seat. If you feel a little dizzy or nauseous, grab a sick bag; the ground crew will be very grateful," he chuckled, as if he knew this was a common occurrence for his 'passengers'.

Andy pressed the small nipple on this oxygen mask again, "Okay." The ground crew removed four large black and yellow taped pins which were then handed to Zychan who secured them in a small storage compartment. "The ejection seats are now live. If you pull either of the two yellow and black handles, above your head or between your legs, we'll be blasted out of here. Only do that if I'm dead and/or the aircraft is about to crash. Otherwise do not touch. Understood?" Andy nodded his understanding rather than try to speak, his heart was racing with excitement, and he didn't want to sound 'goofy' to the experienced pilot.

The ground crew climbed down and detached the ladders from the sides of the aircraft. Zychan pulled the canopy closed and twisted the security handles, locking the cockpit down. From the bubble canopy Andy watched as the ground crew attached a tractor unit to the nose wheel and started to pull the jet-fighter out of the hangar towards the runway. They came to a stop, the tractor unit detached itself and pulled away from the jet.

Sitting in the bright sunlight on the taxi-way Zychan finished his preflight checks and, raising the index finger of his left hand, made two rotations with his finger, said, "It's going to get a little noisy." Andy watched as Zychan applied the wheel brakes then quickly flicked several switches and released a lever then made sure the throttle was pushed forward. Zychan pressed a button and almost immediately the cockpit was filled with a loud whine which turned into a roar as the engines fired up. *Glad I have this helmet on I can only imagine how loud this would be without it!*

"Control this is Yankee Victor two two one, request permission to cross the airfield and move to the take-off position."

"Two two one, you have clearance to move for take-off on runway one eight. Wind is five knots bearing two seven zero degrees."

"Thank you, control." Zychan replied. Andy watched as the ground crew moved and stood in a straight line, well clear of the fighter. The driver of the tractor parked it behind and was the last to join the line. Then Zychan released the wheel brake and as the aircraft moved forward, the ground crew snapped to attention and the Senior NCO of the detail saluted. Zychan responded by tapping the side of his helmet with his right hand to acknowledge them. Using the jet's rudder Zychan moved the aircraft, deftly, to the end of the long runway, then turned to line it up with the bright white lights along the centerline and re-applied the wheel brakes before going through his final checks. He turned to Andy. "Can you check you're strapped in?"

That's a dumb question to ask. They strapped me in not two minutes ago. I'll humor the guy anyway. Andy checked the four webbing-straps still fed into the central buckle positioned above his abdomen. Then he pulled each free end of the webbing to ensure they were done up tightly. "I'm good." Andy replied.

"Control this is Yankee Victor two two one. Request permission to take-off on runway one eight and move into uncontrolled airspace as per my flight plan?"

"Two two one you have permission to take off on runway one eight. Have a safe journey."

"Copy that control, Yankee Victor two two one, out." Zychan released the wheel brake and pulled the throttle back. Andy felt the fighter-jet surge forward, the acceleration pushed him firmly back into his bucket seat. He noticed the white runway lines become a single blur as the jet quickly gathered speed. Long before they reached the end of the runway, the jet climbed into the air. Zychan retracted the landing gear before they had cleared the perimeter of the air base.

Andy felt uneasy as the jet didn't climb as he'd expected. Instead, Zychan kept the aircraft at only a few hundred meters and pushed the fighter faster. He wanted to ask about Zychan's route, but the pilot appeared focused on the ground to their front and the changing icons and images projected onto the head up display. A glance at the air speed indicator showed they were flying at just over eight hundred and fifty miles an hour, the altimeter read they were below three hundred meters in height. The aircraft bucked and shook briefly from thermals as they cleared a series of small hills which Zychan didn't climb higher to clear, instead he held his nerve and stayed at the same altitude.

The ground rose up to meet them, Andy looked to the left and then right as the jet entered a narrow valley, they were flying below the surrounding hills. Farms and livestock flashed by as they pressed on, seconds later the valley opened up to a vast agricultural plain. Zychan banked to the right and then to the left. The aircraft was thrown upwards and then down as they hit another pocket of turbulence, his straps holding him firmly in his seat. He started to feel unusually hot, perspiration ran down his face, he could feel the perspiration on his underarms dripping down his sides. His mind was briefly taken away from his feelings of nausea when Zychan spoke on the radio.

"Hello Kherson control, this is Yankee Victor two two one, request permission to land on runway two one."

"Yankee Victor two two one, we don't have you on our radar. Please confirm your ETA."

"Control, I will have wheels down in thirty seconds unless you want me to do a circuit." To his front, Andy couldn't see the air traffic control tower or any structures to reveal the airport.

"Yankee Victor two two one. You have permission to land on runway two one. Out."
Zychan eased back on the throttle. Andy felt the aircraft immediately respond as the front of the webbing straps exerted more pressure on his chest. Zychan started to lower the flaps. Next, he extended the landing gear and switched on landing lights. In the distance, Andy could see the line of the runway directly in front. To the left were some taller structures and he could just about make out the control tower. Less than fifteen seconds later they were on the ground, Zychan reduced the throttle to an idle and engaged the air brakes slowing the fighter-jet and within a few hundred meters they were nearly stationary. The pilot released the air brakes and applied a small amount of throttle as he directed the aircraft off the runway towards two dark green hangars on a quiet side of the airport.

"We still use this as a military base. Your next ride will be waiting over there." Zychan pointed towards the hangars where Andy could see the spinning rotors of a Russian made Mi-24 helicopter gunship.

"Looks like they're already waiting for me," Andy mused.

"We are worried about the Russians and their activities along our borders. Instability in Moscow means uncertainty within their military which may not be so good for us. An American having a look around can only be a good thing." The fighter jet slowed as it approached the gunship.

"Just because I may see something, doesn't mean I can stop what might happen." Andy replied.

"If there is even a slim chance that you can prevent a war. Then it's worth supporting you." Zychan parked the jet parallel to the gunship. Two ground crew rushed up with a metal ladder and placed it against Andy's side of the aircraft. Two more approached with wheel chocks to stop the jet from moving.

"Thanks for the flight. I really enjoyed it."

"Good luck with your next leg. Stay in the flying suit and leave the helmet with the helicopter crew when they drop you off." Zychan unlocked, then opened the canopy as one of the ground crew appeared over Andy's shoulder and quickly disconnected Andy's oxygen and comms cord. Andy twisted the buckle and pressed it, releasing the four webbing straps which had held him in his seat. Andy stood up and shouted over the noise of the jet engines to the ground crewman that he had a bag in the storage area, while pointing to it. The ground crewman nodded and gave a thumbs up signal to show he understood what Andy had said. Before he climbed down the ladder, Andy gave a friendly pat on Zychan's shoulder and gave him a thumbs up signal of his own.

Andy felt the circulation returning to his legs as he walked quickly towards the gunship. He was relieved when he turned to see the ground crewman running towards him carrying the holdall. Andy held out his hand to receive it. "Thank you!" Andy shouted over the noise. The crewman gave him a thumbs up and turned away.

Andy faced the helicopter and, as he approached it, he ducked below the spinning rotor blades and climbed onboard through the open side door where he was met by the helicopter's air-load master who shouted to him above the screaming noise of the helicopters engines. "Welcome on board, sir, sit there and buckle up." The Senior NCO pointed to the hard seat opposite. "Hand me your bag." Andy didn't want to argue with this no-nonsense woman and handed over his holdall, then buckled up. The air-load master opened a storage bin and placed his holdall in it before closing the bin and checking it was securely closed.

She leaned over Andy and plugged his helmet's comms cord into the helicopter's audio system. Andy could hear the two pilots speaking between themselves about the approaching weather system and what they'd be watching on television that night with their families. The air-load master closed the door and before she had taken her seat, the helicopter climbed and accelerating forward. This time Andy didn't have such a great view as they flew low, skimming just above the treetops. His mind started to wander on what had happened to him over the last twenty-four hours and settled on Lenya.

CHAPTER 16

The air-load master tapped Andy on the arm and brought his attention back to the present leaving the sad thoughts he had of Lenya behind. "Five minutes to the landing zone." He acknowledged her instruction with a thumbs up signal. She continued, "Colonel Andrudski asked me to give you a few items." She held up a sniper's Ghillie suit. "You need to change into this now as it will help keep you concealed when we drop you off. Also a telescopic ladder which I will give to you as you leave."

"Thanks," he replied, giving a thumbs up to confirm he understood in case she wasn't sure.

"Good, now hurry and get into the camouflage clothing." Andy removed his helmet and unbuckled his lap belt, unzipped his flight suit and then spent several frustrating seconds struggling to peel himself out of it. After he managed to extract himself from the flying suit he handed it to the air-load master along with his helmet. Andy unfurled the Ghillie suit onto the floor and quickly unzipped it before picking it up and threaded his legs in, then his arms into the sniper's outfit. As he stood to zip it up, the helicopter moved unexpectedly making him fall back into his seat.

"Thirty seconds to your landing zone," came the call. Andy felt his heart start to race in anticipation of the next part of the mission. *I can do this, calm down, it's just another day at the office. I'm only going to look inside the naval base, nothing else. It's a straightforward plan but I need to be alert.* He stayed seated as he finished zipping himself into the suit. "We won't be landing as the ground is very boggy and slopes, so you will have to jump and roll."

"Okay. Thanks for the warning." Andy shouted back. The air-load master attached a webbing-strap, from her chest harness to an anchor point on the floor and went over to the side door Andy had boarded the helicopter through. She slid it to the right so that it was fully open. Andy felt the cold air blast into the cabin along with the sweet smell of burnt aviation fuel from the helicopters exhaust. He looked through the open doorway at the undulating ground moving quickly by only meters below. She hung out of the doorway looking for obstacles and to the sides as the gunship slowed to a stop and hovered.

"Let's go!" she shouted and gestured for Andy to move towards her. As he reached the open doorway, she turned away and recovered his holdall from the storage bin. He looked down at the long grass below and saw the strands of disruptive material he was wearing dance in the air as the wash from the downdraft blasted him. *Come on Andy. Now or never. Three. Two. One. Go!*

He dropped, keeping his legs together and knees bent waiting for the moment he would land but unsure about how well he would come out of it. Seconds later, he felt his feet hit the ground and he twisted to his left side rolling over his left shoulder. Almost instantly, he felt the cold water from where he touched the waterlogged ground reach his skin. His left side and back were now damp. Andy stood and looked up at the air-load master who was holding his holdall waiting for his signal before she released it. Andy moved below her and she dropped it into his arms. As soon as she released the holdall she disappeared inside the cabin. By the time Andy had placed the holdall on the ground, she was back in position holding the aluminum telescoping ladder. Andy reached up as she released the ladder. Andy placed the ladder next to the holdall. Looking up he saw the air-load master had risen to her feet at which point she gave a thumbs up signal. Andy returned the signal and lowered his body to cover both items. *The last thing I need is this kit being blown into the air and sucked into the engines.*

He heard the gunship's rotors beat faster and the engine noise rose several decibels louder. Andy watched as the gunship climbed less than a meter, edge forwards and slowly make a one-hundred-and-eighty degrees turn. Through the side window he could see the air-load master closing the door from which he'd exited. The gunship picked up speed and, in less than fifteen seconds, was out of his sight, though he could still hear the deep beat from the rotor blades for a good thirty seconds. Once the noise of the helicopter had subsided, Andy was surrounded by silence, save for the sound of a lark singing in the sky above. Andy remained low and did a three-sixty look around. They'd approached from downhill and dropped him in a grassy swamp. To his front, the ground rose slowly at first and then steeply, just over a hundred meters above his current position, the grass gave way to a pine forest which carried on to the ridgeline about a kilometer away. To his right, a gully where a stream flowed down from the forest. To his left, grass with the occasional tussock shrub breaking up the landscape along the side of the hill. Finally, he looked back in the direction the helicopter had flown; the ground flattened out and there were fields planted with corn. About two kilometers away to the right he could see a small copse of trees and, next to the trees, he made out the red iron roof of a farmhouse. Andy worked quickly, putting his right arm through one handle, swinging the bag round to his back before threading his left arm through the other handle and then his hands were free to pick up the telescopic ladder. The ladder was lighter than he'd expected and it had black cord at each end, each tied neatly.

He headed quickly towards the stream along a deep gully which provided perfect cover as he made his way up the stream towards the forest. After a few minutes of careful progress, he entered the pine forest. The going underfoot felt easier the higher he climbed. He stopped for a moment to catch his breath, but also to look and listened to confirm he wasn't being followed or worse, detected. Content there was no one around, Andy approached the small stream and scooped a handful of the cool, clear water and took a few sips before he pressed on the short distance to the ridgeline.

He quickly reached the top of the hill and was disappointed that, despite the climb and height gained, his new vantage point did not offer the clear view of the naval base he'd expected. *Damn! I'm going to have to head down to the edge of the forest and find somewhere to get a clearer view. Not what I needed with the limited time available.*

The ground was steep as he descended and he slipped two or three times on the carpet of pine needles underfoot, having to grab the tree trunks to get a foothold to stop himself from falling. He reached the forest edge which gave way to grassland. The ground to his front continued to descend less steeply to the fence, beyond the fence he could see the perimeter road, a few trees, grassy areas and buildings. He observed that the closer to the water you went, the concentration and size of buildings increased. Here, he was some way out. At this distance, even on the base side of the fence, the chances of the Russians detecting him would be small. However, this position didn't afford good views across the base and he needed to find Crofton.

Andy removed the holdall from his back and placed it onto the floor, then unzipped it to remove his glock. He released the magazine and checked it was still loaded. Satisfied, he returned the magazine into the weapon and placed the pistol into the large chest pocket of his Ghillie suit. Next, he reached in for the full magazines and placed them in the side pockets of his right leg. Finally, he removed the stun-grenade, partially unzipped the front of his Ghillie suit and placed the stun-grenade inside before zipping the suit back up. No matter how much he wanted to get rid of the holdall, it was the easiest way to carry the satellite phone, spare batteries and the laser microphone to his vantage point. *But where?*

He looked around. *Somewhere high with unobstructed views.* His eyes were drawn to a large, dark green metal water tank which stood a good thirty meters above the ground on an iron lattice structure. Two large pipes ran from the tank to the ground and disappeared behind a cluster of large bushes. *On top of the water tank would be perfect.* "But I'd be easily spotted," he said out loud to answer his own thoughts. *The base of the water tank could present a better option ... I need to have a closer look.*

Andy moved cautiously through the open ground, the grass brushing just above his knees. He must have been twenty meters from the fence when a noise carried to him from his right. He stopped. The distinctive sound was of an approaching light utility vehicle traveling along the perimeter road. Its off-road tires running on the tarmac made a high pitched continuous drone. Andy dropped down and lay on his belly in the long grass, the ladder and holdall were by his side and hidden too. He took a quick look at his watch ... *14:30.*

The sound of the military vehicle grew louder and with each passing second his heart beat faster. He fought hard against the impulsive urge to rise up and look at the vehicle. The Russian patrol were close, but their vehicle didn't slow as it cruised past his position. Andy waited for the drone of the patrol vehicle to fade to silence as it continued with its sweep of the perimeter. He turned his body towards the direction the patrol had headed, then listened to the silence for a few seconds to be certain they had gone.

Satisfied he was alone, he pulled the hood of the Ghillie suit over his head to break-up his outline and keep him invisible. Andy slowly lifted his upper body to see above the tall grass. The perimeter road was clear. Rising to his feet he grabbed the holdall with one hand and the ladder with the other then made his way to the high metal fence with its sharp tipped posts. Andy put the holdall down, fully extended the ladder and placed it upright against the fence. The extended ladder reached almost to the top of the fence. Andy smiled, he knew that using the ladder he could easily clear the fence. *But how to take the ladder with me?*

That's when it struck him that he should use the cord attached to the ladder. He climbed up and untied the cord at the top of the ladder and wrapped it around his right wrist, finishing it off with a simple knot. Satisfied the cord wouldn't come undone at the wrong moment, he bent down and grabbed the holdall in his left hand. Then, with one last look around to check he was still alone, he placed his foot on the first rung of the ladder and continued upwards as fast as he could. The ladder bounced slightly with each powerful stride and, on reaching the top rung, he launched himself upwards easily clearing the top of the perimeter fence.

As the effects of gravity took over, he brought his right arm up above his head, then moved his arm as far forward as he could, pulling hard on the cord. The lightweight ladder leapt upwards as he fell towards the ground. It looked almost choreographed as the bottom of the ladder cleared the top of the fence at the same time Andy hit the ground and rolled while focused on protecting the delicate contents of the holdall.

Andy's feeling of satisfaction changed to panic as he realized the ladder was attached to him and the tension on the cord had pulled it towards him. The falling ladder made a direct bee-line for him. Keeping the tension off the cord he rolled out of the path of the ladder as it crashed to the ground with a clatter. Andy quickly untied the knot to release the cord from his wrist, then rolled it up and secured it before he collapsed the ladder. Whilst still crouched, he took the opportunity to look around again to check he was not being watched. Then he stood upright, grabbed the holdall and ladder, and headed to the base of the water tank.

Less than five minutes later he lay on the ground under the shadow of a large bush, the snipers suit made him invisible amongst the foliage and tall grasses. The ladder remained concealed by the grass as it lay further back, just out of arms reach in a small indentation in the ground. Andy edged further back and rolled onto his side then opened the holdall. The first item he touched were a pair of palm sized binoculars with rubber hand grips. He reached for them and placed them to one side. Next, he found the laser microphone and using two hands he carefully removed it and placed it next to the binoculars. He had to rummage in the holdall to find the headphones with their padded black leather ear cuffs. Andy grabbed the three items and edged forward again to scan the naval base below. *Perfect!*

There were convoys of soft skinned troop transporters moving slowly and converging on the main parade square where four columns of armored personnel carriers and three columns of T72 Main Battle Tanks lined up. Their crews were armed and sat lazing around. *Probably awaiting their orders.* Nothing leapt out at him to indicate Crofton's whereabouts. He picked up the binoculars and methodically swept the scene from right to left. During his second sweep he found Crofton's motorcycle parked outside the Officers' Mess. Andy adjusted the focus on the binoculars and peered through each of the Mess windows. He could see uniformed figures moving in the two windows to the right of the main entrance … *but no Crofton!*

CHAPTER 17

"What have we here?" he whispered to himself. He put the binoculars down and pushed the headphone's jack plug into the socket at the base of the handle for the microphone. The laser microphone looked like a cut down rifle, it had a stock, optical sight and what looked to be a short, fat barrel, which Andy knew to be the laser and detector. The optical sight wasn't as powerful as the optics on the binoculars, but now he'd found what he was looking for, the set-up from the microphone's optics would give a reasonable view of the Officers' Mess. He switched the unit on and pointed the dot from the lasers red indicator at the window where he'd seen the activity. Instantly he could hear voices engaged in conversation.

"... surprisingly well, with no push back from the Government of the United States."

A second voice cut in, "Do you think they know?"

A third male voice spoke, this one had an American accent, "Of course they do! Our people in Langley have suppressed much of the data they've gathered and, on the ground, we've taken active measures to blind them." *Crofton?* Andy could feel a surge of anger rising within and his heart beat faster.

A senior staff officer in a naval uniform approached the window, Andy could see his lips move as he spoke, a fraction of a second later he could hear his words. "Excellent, this is good news, our forces here are ready to push forward in co-ordination with the Army Battle Groups to the East." A man in dark clothing approached the window to stand next to the Naval officer, Andy clearly saw his face, it was Crofton.

Crofton spoke next, "We have military cameramen in place to film footage at key locations which will provide good optics for us. I also have a production team waiting, they'll stitch it together and we'll send the footage to Moscow for broadcast on all major channels. The Prime Minister will publicly support the invasion of the Ukraine as our units move in to secure the Kremlin and remove the President from office. The Prime Minister will declare a state of emergency and with his Parliament's support, claim the office of the President."

Another, quieter voice, spoke and Andy had to listen hard to hear, "I have coordinated with several nationalist groups in Moscow and, when the invasion is broadcast, they will take to the streets in support of the invasion and the Prime Minister. They will also take action to prevent the police, and any military units loyal to the President, from making progress through the city to assist the deposed President."

"When do the others arrive?" the naval officer asked.

"Within the hour." Crofton replied. *I've heard enough.* Andy put the laser microphone down, moved back to the holdall, removing the satellite dish, base transceiver and handset with its long black coaxial cable. He unfurled the lightweight mesh dish, set up its tripod and positioned it outside the bush line, pointing south, before connecting the dish to the base transceiver and twisting the plug into the socket until it gave a reassuring *'click'*. Next, he connected the handset. Satisfied each of the components were correctly connected, Andy pushed the power button and waited.

Several seconds later the transceiver unit came to life and started its boot up sequence. the units green *'Signal Strength Indicator'* light flashed slowly. Andy adjusted the mesh dish to the right, then stopped, the green light was now flashing quickly. He moved the dish another ten degrees to the right and stopped;

the green light was continuous. *Good ... at least I'm talking to the satellite.* Andy looked at the control panel of the base transceiver unit where he saw a flashing prompt for him to enter his '*Access Code*'. Andy entered the code and the unit flashed '*READY*'. Andy punched in the country code and number for Ross. He held the handset close and listened as the line fell silent for a few seconds and then he heard the far end ringing. It stopped ringing as a voice came on the line.

"Hello, Jamie Ross."

"Hi Jamie, it's Andy from sunny Sevastopol," he whispered.

"They got you there?"

"Yes and I've found Crofton."

"In the base?"

"Yes, in the Officers' Mess would you believe? He's meeting with unidentified others."

"Be careful, you know he's dangerous." *She sounds genuinely concerned,* he thought. It wasn't what he was expecting, as she continued, "What have you learned?"

"They are preparing to invade the Ukraine from the South and East. The invasion is to appeal to nationalists in Moscow. It's all part of a plot to depose the Russian President. The plan is to replace him with the Prime Minister."

"We can't sit on this. Do you know anyone in Moscow we could bring in?"

Andy thought for a moment. "Yes I do, Ambassador Rushbrooke, he's well connected, in both Washington and Moscow."

"Why not Carrie Roper?"

"She'll refer it straight back to Langley and Crofton will find out. The Ambassador is outside of the agency and unlikely to be our leak, plus he can easily reach senior leaders in both Russia and our own Government."

"You know the Ambassador?" she couldn't hide the tone of incredulity in her voice.

"Yes, I've met him a few times and he's helped me on a field operation. I think he'll help."

"Okay, bring him in." Ross said with some hesitation. Andy hit the *'Create Conference'* button on the touchscreen and dialed the Ambassador's direct line. The call was answered after two rings.

"Ambassador Rushbrooke." His voice sounded distant. *Not a brilliant line.*

"Ambassador, it's Andy Flint. I'm using a satellite phone, so there will be delays and the quality won't be great." There was a pause while the Ambassador either racked his brain to remember who Andy was, or the line had delays.

"Understood. Hey, I heard they moved you out of Moscow. Where are you?"

"I'm in the Russian naval base at Sevastopol on the Black Sea in the Ukraine. I'm overlooking the base right now."

"What are you doing there? This time are you looking to help an Admiral defect?" Rushbrooke laughed.

"Nothing like that. I'm just going to bring Jamie Ross into this call. She's the agency lead in Kiev."

"Go ahead son."

Andy pressed the *'Join Callers'* button on the touchscreen. The ear piece on the handset quietly beeped twice. "Ambassador Rushbrooke, Jamie Ross is now on the line. I'm calling from the Russian naval base at Sevastopol. I'm in a covert location observing a meeting between senior Russian military officers and a former CIA field agent, John Crofton."

"Okay Andy. Why am I on this call?" The Ambassador wanted to quickly get down to business.

"There's a Russian military buildup just across the border from the Ukraine. Also, the naval base here is gearing up to form part of the invasion force. The Russian Government denies any knowledge of the build-up, that's because, from what I've just heard, they don't know."

"Andy, I think you're right, they'd never sanction an invasion of the Ukraine with all of their domestic problems they have today." Andy connected a cable between the laser microphone and the satellite transceiver as the Ambassador continued, "In addition, President Yeltsin needs all of the support he can get from the West, an invasion of the Ukraine would leave him more isolated."

"Can we warn the Russian Government?" Ross asked. Andy heard the Ambassador take a deep breath.
"Miss Ross, I serve only at the pleasure of our President. This is such a big call, only he can make that decision. Please wait while I make that call." With the Ambassador out from the call, Andy used the time to direct the laser microphone back at the window of the Officers' Mess and listen through one ear while with the other, he continued to listen to the satellite call.

"...and our approach to military prisoners? Do we detain or kill them?" A voice asked.

"We detain them. We will no doubt have some of our own men captured and, later, there will need to be a prisoner exchange as part of any negotiated settlement."

"Good. I'll make sure this instruction is covered in the orders our troops receive."

The satellite handset made a popping sound. The Ambassador returned to the conference call. "Miss Ross, Mr. Flint, I have the

President on the line." *What!*

CHAPTER 18

Even while in the middle of a dangerous operation inside enemy territory, Andy felt his heart race with excitement at the thought of speaking with the President of the United States. Rushbrooke spoke first, "Mr. President, thank you for giving your time at such short notice to join our call, I wouldn't have brought you in unless I had to."

"Understood. I'd been told just before I jumped on this conference call that the Russians are preparing to invade the Ukraine and their Government doesn't know about it. We have a man on the ground inside the Russian naval base in Sevastopol watching it all go down."

Andy interrupted. "Yes, Mr. President, the invasion is part of a plan to initiate a coup against President Yeltsin."

"Brent, what do you know about this?" *Wait, Brent Scowcroft the President's National Security Adviser, is on the line too!*

"Mr. President, as you know from your daily briefings, things are unstable in Russia. They have a standoff between President Yeltsin and the Parliament. We believe the military are staying out of this, but we do see their forces massing on the border with the Ukraine, however, we do not know of their intent. It could be just an exercise."

Rushbrooke interrupted. "The Russian Government doesn't even know that their forces are gathering on the border with Ukraine. I spoke with them only two days ago about this very topic. Told me to my face I was wrong!"

"You believe they don't know?" The President asked.

"Yes Mr. President, I do." Rushbrooke replied.

"Yeltsin said the very same thing to me too, when I spoke with him last week, but why invade?" the President asked.

Rushbrooke answered, "An invasion would animate the nationalists across Russia, boosting support for Yeltsin's opponents and forcing the military to take a side. In my opinion, after an invasion, they'd back the nationalists."

Scowcroft added. "Mr. President, we have no evidence that the build up by the Russians is nothing more than preparation for a military exercise. This happens all the time."

Andy pressed the '*Add External Feed*' key on the satellite transceiver to connect what he was hearing to the conversation, "... without air cover our forces will be vulnerable" came a voice from the meeting in the Officers' Mess.
"The Commander-in-Chief doesn't want to play any part in a change of Government, regardless of his personal feelings about the direction Yeltsin is taking our nation."

"But you couldn't even secure ground attack fighters," the first speaker countered.

"General Deynekin is a popular commander. His officers are fiercely loyal to him ... they would not act without his orders," replied the second voice.

Another speaker, this one with a deeper voice joined the conversation, "Make sure he is quickly replaced by someone who supports us."

"What do we do without close air support?" the first voice asked.

A fourth speaker joined the conversation, "We have an air defense regiment within our orbat. At H-hour minus four we will activate our air defense systems and create a shield within mother Russia and from our vessels here. Once we cross into the Ukraine, our mobile air defense batteries will push forward to positions which we have already identified, here, here and here." *They must be looking at a map.* "Our forces will be safe from any attack coming from the air. In addition, our air defense units will stop the Ukrainians from moving their troops by air; if they do they'll be shot out of the sky."

President Clinton spoke, "Okay, I've heard enough, Brent, the Russian military is clearly readying for an invasion but not everyone is behind them. I've made my mind up."

"Mr. President, I'd like to receive your direction." Rushbrooke asked.

"Martin, get the Russian President on the line. If you can't get him on to hear what's happening in his own naval base, then maybe I can."

"Yes Mr. President. I'll call him now." Rushbrooke replied. Andy disconnected the external feed from the microphone. In the distance he could hear the sound of a Russian light utility vehicle making its way around the perimeter road. He looked at his watch. *That was quick. I wasn't expecting them for another forty minutes. I'll be safe, in this position they can't see me from the perimeter track.*

Moments later another voice came onto the line. Andy thought he recognized it. "Mr. President, I don't believe it's in our best interests to make the Russian President aware of what his military are doing."

"James, I know you spooks have your own agenda and deposing governments, maybe starting World War Three, is possibly one of them. But I can't leave the Russian President hang out to dry!" *I thought I recognized the voice, James Woolsey, our new Director.* Andy recalled his graduation ceremony at Langley, Woolsey attended to present the awards and make a speech. Andy liked him.

"Mr. President, all this domestic upheaval in Russia is giving us access to assets and information which comes about only when there is uncertainty and insecurity. Senior officials, with information, want to trade. When times are good, and there is stability, they have no need to seek us out. I recommend keeping the Russian Government in the dark and letting this play out."

"You spooks are always up to something. James is there anything you're not telling me which I should be aware of?"

"Mr. President. All I can say is that my advisers tell me we have a large number of sensitive operations running in Russia and your olive branch to this weak Russian Government may jeopardize the lives of our brave field agents."

"That's a nice speech," the President responded dryly.

Rushbrooke came back onto the conference call, "Mr. President, Mr. Woolsey, Mr. Scowcroft, I have President Yeltsin on the line. He's now in this conference call."

"Bill, what is the reason for Ambassador Rushbrooke's unexpected call?"

"Boris, I'm sorry to interrupt you with this call, but this matter is important to both of us and it concerns your forces massing on the border with the Ukraine."

Andy heard a loud sigh from Yeltsin, "Look Bill, I've told you and your people, we do not have any forces massing on the borders with the Ukraine. Also, I have not issued any orders to invade anyone. I am still in command of all Russian military and strategic nuclear forces. Please take my reassurances to be true. You have my word."

President Clinton continued, "Mr. Flint is an American field agent currently located inside your naval base at Sevastopol and he's watching a meeting taking place right now; he's got a listening device pointed to it, Mr. Flint, if you could work your magic please."

"Yes, Mr. President."

Andy touched the display and, immediately, voices from the meeting in the Officers' Mess could be heard on the conference call.
"... H-hour remains unchanged at 2am. H-hour plus four, we should have secured all of our strategic objectives, and the Ukrainian Government will be waking up to our forces occupying Odessa, Crimea, Dnipro and Kharkiv, almost cutting the country in two. We have our agitators gathered in Kiev ready to protest in support of the occupation."

A second voice spoke, "Our military media units will be filming our troops advancing and crushing Ukrainian resistance; the edited highlights will be ready for broadcast in Moscow for the morning news shows."
The deep voice came back into the conversation, "The Prime Minister is aware of the plans and will make a rousing speech to his constituents on national television. He's scheduled to be there for the morning's seven o'clock broadcast; he'll be arriving at six to avoid any street disturbances or police roadblocks. After his broadcast goes out, I'll appeal to the other senior military commanders who aren't yet on our side."

"That's Gromov!" Yeltsin exploded, "He's in command of my navy ... the traitor."

Andy could hear the sound of a heavy truck making its way slowly around the base perimeter road but, with an important conference call to focus on, he chose to ignore it. *I'm concealed and they won't see me.*

"Get me my head of Military Intelligence and the FSB!" Yeltsin bellowed in the background.

"By H-hour plus six President Yeltsin will be struggling to stay ahead of the news cycle. By H-hour plus seven he will have lost control of his military as our tanks arrive to contain him. Our troops will take him into protective custody and we will fly him here. By the time he lands, he will have lost all authority and we will have a new President."

"Mr. Flint, I think we've heard enough. Please disconnect that." President Clinton ordered. Andy touched the *'Disconnect External Feed'* button on the screen severing the audio from the Officers' Mess.
"Boris, it's Bill, do you now believe what we're telling you? You have rogue elements within your military who are planning to invade the Ukraine and play a part in a coup against you?"

"I can't believe what I've just heard. Those treacherous dogs are going against me and the democratic wishes of our people. I'm going to have to sit down and have a stiff drink to calm my nerves."

Andy watched as two Russian Hind gunships, flying low and in close formation from the East, flew to Andy's front, coming to a halt above a grassed area next to the Officers' Mess where they hovered for a few seconds. Crofton appeared at the Mess door accompanied by a senior naval officer, he descended the steps to face the two gunships and gave the signal to land, in response, they started their slow descent, landing together on the grass. "Mr. President, I have more senior VIPs arriving for the meeting at the Officers' Mess, they've arrived in two military gunships."

Yeltsin spoke next, "Thank you Bill. Thank you Mr. Flint. My advisers are here; we'll deal with things in our own way."

President Clinton replied. "Good luck Boris."

Andy heard a click on the line as President Yeltsin dropped off the call. However, another new voice came onto the line. A voice Andy hadn't heard before, "Mr. Flint, I'm Edward Charles the third, Director Special Operations at the CIA. Where exactly are you?"

"I'm inside the Russian naval base at Sevastopol" Andy answered.

"Are you there as part of an on-going operation sanctioned by my department or anyone at the CIA?" Charles sounded combative. *What the fuck? He wants to throw me under a bus and discredit me.*

"I was inside the Luhansk station when Crofton blew it up. I was there when he attacked my apartment and killed my girlfriend. As part of my investigation into those murders we tracked a motorcycle which was at both those incidents, and that's what brought me here. Now, we have concrete evidence of plans, from rogue members of the Russian military, to invade the Ukraine and start a coup in Russia," Andy paused for a split second while they took in what he'd said. "So, with the President and the National Security Adviser on the line, do you want to tell me that my being here is a bad idea?"

"Listen Flint. We're part of a big team and we all have a position to play. You have to play in yours and not go all maverick on your own."

"Mr. Charles, this is Ambassador Rushbrooke, without Mr. Flint being there we wouldn't have learned any of this, or did you already know and were keeping this from your own government?" Charles fell silent for some seconds before he continued.

"I have to keep my deep cover agents and sources safe. You may have just cost some of them their lives."

"And Mr. Flint may have just saved the Russian Government from being overthrown in a nationalistic coup and invasion of a friendly nation." Rushbrooke replied.

Andy saw the red battery warning light flashing on the transceiver unit. "Mr. President, I'm sorry I have to bring this call to an early finish as the battery on my satellite phone needs to be changed. I can be back on line in a few minutes if you want to reconvene."

"Mr. Flint, I think we are done on this call. Brent, I'll expect an update from you later on today. If Boris calls and asks for any assistance, you make sure he gets it. Okay team go and make a difference today. One last thing. Andy, you don't need to be told you're doing a great job."

Ouch! A very public slap down for the Director of Special Operations! "Thank you, Mr. President"

Andy ended the call and slowly edged himself backwards to the satellite transceiver and holdall. He powered down the transceiver unit, removed its battery and unzipped the holdall so he could switch the battery for a fully charged one. To identify the discharged battery he looked in the holdall for a marker pen or a piece of cord; nothing. He looked around, pulled a long piece of grass from the ground and tied it around the used battery before he placed it in the holdall and removed one of the two fully charged batteries. Once he'd attached the new battery to the satellite transceiver he pressed the unit's power button. The *Signal Strength Indicator* light flashed and then became continuous. With his communications back up and available, Andy slowly edged forwards to his observation post.

It was then he heard it, the faint sound of movement carried to him as someone walked through the tall grass. *Shit!* In his excitement at being on a call with the President he'd forgot to keep checking around him and realized that ignoring the vehicles he'd heard had been a mistake. He remained motionless, hoping that the sound would disappear but it didn't go away, it just got louder. *Someone's walking nearby. It's more than one person. It's a patrol?*

Andy touched his zip in readiness to reach for his glock when a new sound reached him. The sound of a rifle being cocked. Andy's heart race. He wanted to turn and look, however, before he could move a Russian voice spoke, "You in the camouflage clothing. Put your hands up. Now!" The sound of more rifles being readied made Andy freeze. He slowly raised his hands.

CHAPTER 19

With his hands raised above his head, Andy rose slowly to his feet and turned to face the direction from where the commands were coming. Immediately in front of him were eight soldiers dressed in green combat uniforms, their faces hidden by green balaclavas worn underneath their helmets. They were pointing their assault rifles directly at his chest. In his peripheral vision, to his right, he could see a second squad of soldiers sweeping through the area. In the background, the heavy truck and the light utility vehicle he'd heard and ignored were parked up. *Damn.*

"Keep your hands raised and walk towards me," the squad leader commanded. Andy followed his instructions. "Stop and get down onto your knees. Place your hands behind your back." Placing his hands behind his back he was puzzled. *How the hell did they find me? I had a great position and I was all but invisible in this suit.*

One of the other soldiers standing to the side lowered his weapon and approached him without stepping in front of his squad. Andy saw the soldier produce a black plastic zip-tie from his jacket breast pocket just as the soldier left his view moving behind his back. Andy felt the zip-tie tighten around his wrists, then, at the last second the soldier pulled it tight, making the zip-tie bite into his skin. His world was the plunged into darkness as the soldier pulled a thick black cotton hood over his head. Andy tried to see though the hood, hoping to catch even a faint glimmer of light, but without success.

"Bring him to the truck." The squad leader ordered. Andy felt a pair of hands firmly grip his upper arms and pull him to his feet. A hand held his right arm and guided him forwards. While Andy walked cautiously over the uneven ground, the squad leader continued to issue orders to his men. "You two, bring his equipment and check the area to make sure he hasn't hidden anything nearby."

Next, and most chillingly, Andy heard the squad leader talking on a radio. "Gold Command, we have acquired the target. Exactly where you said." Andy's mind spun. *How? Sure I was a bit careless by dismissing the vehicles, but, if you were already looking for me, who tipped you off?*
"Yes, sir, we will. Out." He heard the metal tailgate on the rear of the heavy truck crash loudly as it dropped down. Seconds later, he heard at least two soldiers climbing up the tailgate into the rear of the truck.

"Help him into the truck," the squad leader ordered. Andy felt hands roughly grab his upper arms and pull him upwards as another pair of hands gripped his waist and lifted him. He was momentarily winded when his chest made a heavy contact with the rear edge of the flat back of the truck. The soldiers dragged him over the metal ridged floor, his knees taking a pounding. Suddenly, he was propelled forwards, making him momentarily airborne as the hands let go.
What goes up, has got to come down. Andy tensed in anticipation of his landing. He wasn't disappointed when he crashed heavily onto the hard metal floor; his head struck with a painful crack, the far end of the cargo compartment. He was stunned and saw an instantaneous bright flash of light. His head whipped back as he crumpled to the floor. With his hands secured behind his back and lying in a twisted heap on the floor of the truck, Andy listened to the sounds of more soldiers climbing into the back of the truck to join him. His head throbbed with pain and he was on the verge of unconsciousness. *Stay awake, I need to stay awake!*

"Dimitri, do you still think this is an exercise when we find a camouflaged soldier with sophisticated gear watching the camp?"

"Ivan I'm starting to believe your theory that this is for real" a second voice responded.

"You two stop talking and keep a close watch on the prisoner," the squad leader shouted from outside the truck.

"Yes corporal," one of the men responded. Then, in a quiet conspiratorial tone, "Since his promotion, Mikhail has changed, wanker!" The men in the truck laughed nervously.

From the loud crashing of metal against metal, the rattling of chains and the sliding of metal pins, Andy figured the tailgate had been raised and secured into place. He heard the sound of an engine firing up. *The light vehicle.* Then the truck shook and vibrated wildly as its engine started. As they lurched forwards, he felt himself slide back an inch along the floor of the truck, that's when the soles of four combat boots pressed down on his back, pinning him to the floor.

The truck slowly made its way around the rest of the perimeter track and deep into the base. Andy could hear shouts from outside the truck at intervals but could not make out what was being shouted above the noise from the truck. He focused his energy on trying to work out other sounds he could hear. *I need to stay alert.* There were vehicles, lots of different ones, some like this truck, but others emitted deeper, throatier sounds. These vehicles were far more powerful. *Armored units.*

Andy felt the truck pull to a stop and heard a door open. He heard someone climb down from the cab and the footfall of combat boots moving along the left side towards the rear of the truck. The boots which had pressed down him lifted away, then two pairs of hands grabbed him roughly and pulled him to his feet as he heard the sound of the tailgate being released and dropped causing the chains to rattle. He heard soldiers alighting from the truck before he was pulled towards the tailgate and he figured he must be near the edge as there was a slight pause so he prepared to be roughly alighted. However, without warning the hands released him and he felt a boot in the small of his back propelling him forwards out of the truck. *What the...I hope they catch me.*

He felt himself falling, so prepared as best he could for an impact he knew was going to be painful, and then he hit the tarmac with a dull thud. His head struck the hard surface almost knocking him unconscious. The wind was knocked out of him and he struggled to catch his breath, the stun-grenade, which was still tucked down the front of his Ghillie suit, may have broken a few ribs as he hit the ground. He tasted blood in his mouth. *Thanks guys appreciate your help.*

"You idiots! Don't kill him; that's my job!" barked a new voice, Andy was immediately alerted to the Russian being spoken had a trace of an American accent, "Pick him up! Where's the gear he had with him? Bring that too!" Two pairs of hands picked him up and, without giving him time to get to his feet, pulled him forwards, his legs dragging behind scuffing the toes of his boots on the tarmac.

He heard soldiers marching alongside him, the rhythm of the steps in unison clear above the other noises around him. Andy winced in pain as his shins struck a step, he instinctively raised his knees, but not high enough to prevent his feet from striking the next step. *That hurt!* Andy pulled his knees higher keeping his feet safe. He felt the soldiers drag him to the right and he noticed the sounds around him change. They were inside a building and he was being dragged along on a carpeted floor. They made another right turn and he sensed they had brought him to a larger room. *The Officers' Mess?* Thick cigarette smoke stung his eyes and burnt his throat which indicated he was right. He now had the opportunity to orientate himself by recalling the layout of the air base.

"Put his gear on the table," the American ordered. "Oh it's a satellite system. Set it up and let's see how good the CIA's latest comms equipment is." Andy heard someone behind him unzipped his holdall and manhandle the equipment, snapping of connectors into place as they assembled his equipment. "Take off the hood." A hand gripped the top of the hood and pulled it off taking a clump strands of hair with it, he winced. The bright lights blinded Andy making him blink repeatedly to adjust to the light. When things settled down, he found himself standing in front of a small group of military staff officers and, right in the middle, John Crofton.

CHAPTER 20

"Mr. Andrew Flint of the CIA, welcome, I can see my friends have already introduced themselves," Crofton pointed at each of the guards who stood on either side of him.

"John Crofton, missing presumed dead, now alive and kicking." Crofton had a similar height and build to Andy and wore a para-military style uniform: black combat boots, camouflage pants and a dark green tee-shirt with some form of crest printed in black over his heart. *That will make him look the part, I guess.* The look was completed with the obligatory pistol strapped in a holster to his right thigh.

"As you see, I'm not dead. I hope you don't believe everything the CIA tells you." Crofton's attention switched to the soldiers assembling the satellite equipment. "Why have you stopped?"

"It's asking for an access code."

"Ah, password protected? Now then Mr. Flint, it's time for you to do your stuff, and help yourself at the same time. if you will do the honors, please." Crofton gestured with his open hand towards the assembled equipment behind him. Andy turned and wasn't surprised to see his satellite equipment; the small parabolic dish was set-up on the grass outside with its black coaxial cable feeding through an open window. "I'd like to show off your latest technology to our audience, plus, I haven't spoken with my mom in quite some time. I think she'll be surprised to receive my call," he said with force laughter and looked around at the officers who took this as their cue to join in.

Andy didn't move or say anything in response to the command. Then, clearly annoyed with Andy's lack of movement he repeated his command at the same time nodding at the two guards who roughly pushed Andy in the direction of the table. Still not making any move to 'help', Crofton stood behind him and shouted, "Enter the damn code!"

Andy decided to make some effort, he was still working out what sort of person Crofton was, and if he was to live past the next minute, moving towards the table was going to be a good idea. However, when he reached the table, he stopped and flexed his hands open and closed rapidly to show they were still bound. "Untie him. What do you think he will do with all of you surrounding him and another ten thousand combat-ready troops sat outside?" *Clearly you aren't a patient man, and whatever is going on, has you stressed big time. I wonder what you're like under real pressure.* With the zip-tie cut free, Andy turned to face the satellite transceiver and keyed in the access code. He saw the indicator light turn solid green. *They have the satellite.*

"It's working, Sir," announced a junior NCO's excited. Andy turned to face Crofton.
"Good. Now Mr. Flint, you are quite an irritant and, I must say, I'm impressed that you're still alive. You remind me of a cat with nine lives, but I think, today, you have used them all up."

"As they say, never count your chickens," Andy countered and smiled. The Russians around Crofton looked puzzled as the nuances of the conversation were lost on them.

"I will say that for someone so young you've made quite an impression. You stole the Politburo Minutes from within the official archives, right under the noses of the Russians, then you went on to manage the defection of Colonel Shanina against the direction of the Agency." *What? Wait, how did you learn this? You had disappeared from the agency long before any of this happened.*

"The death of Tex was clearly a tragic accident. That must have hit you hard. A bit like the loss of your team in Luhansk."

Andy felt rage rising inside of him and placed his hands behind his back and clenched his hands into tight fists. "You murdered my girlfriend you bastard!" Andy spat out as he lunged at Crofton with his arms outstretched reaching for Crofton's throat. But the guards were too quick, saw Andy's move, and grabbed his arms, stopping him in his tracks.

"Calm down. You'll be joining her soon enough," Crofton called out as he faced off against Andy. "Tell me. Why are you here? Langley certainly didn't sanction your little covert activity here today."

You are way too well informed, who are you working with on the inside and what have you got over them that my every move has been fed to you in such detail. "First tell me how you found me?"

Crofton sneered. "Oh that was easy. The moment you switched on that Satellite phone, your GPS co-ordinates were automatically broadcast to Langley who kindly informed me that a CIA transmission system had activated somewhere nearby. They even provided your exact co-ordinates, which I think was very generous of them.

"Why would they do that?"

"You really are fresh out of The Farm; you haven't seen what's really going on at all, have you?"

Andy was completely confused. Crofton carried on, "The American Government is divided into those who get elected every five years and appeal to the masses for their votes. They take a short term, opportunistic view of America and the world. They only seek one thing, to get re-elected or make their name in the history books. None of this is good for America or its people. That's why there is a second part to the Government. The patriotic men and women who serve a greater good regardless of the transient administration holding office. We're known as Torchbearers. We Torchbearers have only one interest and that's to protect America. But to protect America, we need a strong military. We need a strong security and law enforcement apparatus."

Andy continued to look puzzled. "So why are you here in the Ukraine, in a Russian naval base about to start an invasion and topple one, possibly two governments?"

"Instability within the Russia Government and their military aggressively seizing territory will only help our cause. We'll see increased funding for better military equipment, for more troops, more airmen and a big increase in the capability of our navy."

"You're mad."

"You just don't understand. We've been quietly working in the background for over a hundred and fifty years creating global instability so we can keep our military forces well-funded, equipped and trained. Why do you think the CIA regularly acts in ways which only create bigger problems for our nation to solve? Because when the US government sends in its military, our interventions require a big response, which sees our military and intelligence services committed for years. Which is what we are seeking to happen here in Eastern Europe."

"You really are mad." Andy repeated. At least one of the Russians behind Crofton nodded in agreement. The sound of panicked shouting from outside of the Officers' Mess made the room fall quiet. One of the naval officers spoke first, "I'll find out what's going on." Before he had a chance to move, the ear splitting sound of an air raid siren wailed mournfully outside. Seconds later more sirens joined in, the noise deafening. The naval officer ran towards the door and headed outside. A telephone attached to the wall started to ring, second naval officer picked it up placed his index finger into his free ear to reduce the sound of the sirens while he attempted to hear what he was being told.

The officer shouted down the phone to have the message repeated more than once. He didn't have to wait to hear the full message, as the deep clattering sounds of rotor blades from approaching helicopters could now be heard over the wail of the air raid sirens, and bursts of heavy machine gunfire added to the chaos.

"We're under attack!" the officer replaced the handset.

"Get out there, lead your troops and defend this base!" the senior naval officer in the room ordered. An instant later the open window shattered, throwing glass fragments into the room. Andy winced with pain as shards of glass struck his back. He turned to look at the broken window in time to see the two gunships parked on the lawn being strafed by heavy machine gun fire from an airborne Russian gunship moving at low level slowly from across the far side of the parade square. Of his two guards, one lay twitching on the floor, a large pool of blood gathered under him as blood pumped from a large neck wound. *He's on his way out.* The second guard lifted up his left arm. His left hand was missing two fingers; Andy could see a third finger held only by tendons hanging down by his wrist. The guard looked pale and preoccupied with his injuries. *He's no threat.*

Andy quickly turned his attention back to the room where Officers, who'd only moments before stood with Crofton, were running for the exits, thinning the room. Crofton remained behind issuing instructions to an Officer wearing a flying suit. Andy unzipped the front of his Ghillie suit and reached for the flash bang. Squeezing the handle while he clasped the grenade with his right hand, he pulled the pin with his left and tossed it towards Crofton who only noticed the grenade when it landed and clattered over the floor towards him. Andy turned away and put his index fingers into his ears to reduce the sound of the explosion. The back wall he was looking at lit up and, not only did he hear it detonate, he felt the concussion from the explosion against his back pushing him forward. Andy reached into his chest pocket for the glock while turning to face Crofton.

Crofton wasn't where he'd been stood only moments earlier. The pilot who had been speaking with Crofton, staggered unsteadily on his feet as the flash had blinded him and the bang concussed him. Then he saw Crofton, he had already reached the rooms rear exit. By the time Andy raised the pistol to fire, Crofton had slipped through the open door. Andy squeezed off two rounds in a rapid double tap, punching large holes in the back wall where he expected Crofton might be heading. Andy knew he'd broken many CIA rules in the last few hours, and now he'd broken one of the first principles of marksmanship: being able to see your target before pulling the trigger. *Hell no! Crofton isn't getting away from me regardless of who else might get hurt along the way, this is for Lenya.*

Andy was determined to bring Crofton down. Holding his pistol firmly in his right hand and aimed at chest height, Andy took off after Crofton pausing briefly at the doorway as he scanned for threats. Then, from his right, the hand of an unseen assailant pushed the pistol upwards. Andy was taken by surprise, he hadn't expected Crofton to try and ambush him so early. A fist slammed into his chest, the recent damage to his ribs amplified the pain which shot throughout his body like a surge of electricity. The force of the punch stopped him in his tracks.

Crofton grappled with Andy's wrist trying to break his tight grip on the pistol. Crofton slammed Andy's hand with the pistol against the door frame three times in the hope that it would become dislodged. Andy turned to face Crofton, who was leaning forward and using his bodyweight to push Andy backwards, and head-butted Crofton right on the bridge of his nose causing Crofton to recoil in pain, but not-enough to stop him releasing a powerful right connecting with the side of Andy's face. The blow stung and knocked Andy off-balance briefly. He forced himself to keep hold of the glock as he crashed into the door frame.

Andy saw a kick coming and before it made contact, he threw himself backwards through the open door into the main room he'd been held in. At the same instant that his back hit the floor, he fired four rounds into the wall hoping at least one would make contact with some part of Crofton. Andy's chest stung like hell and he struggled to breathe as he got to his feet. The room was empty save for the dead guard. *His injured buddy has probably gone for help ... or just run off to save his own skin...* Andy moved towards the open doorway, this time more cautiously, and seeing it was clear turned right into a corridor and ran along it until he reached a junction.

He looked right, and saw the corridor went twenty meters and came to a dead end. Then he looked left, twenty meters along was an exit sign and at the end of the corridor a fire door only this was open. He ran towards the fire door and fired a round to the right and a round to the left of the doorway just in case Crofton was waiting in ambush again. He burst through the doorway in time to see Crofton running around the side of the building near the parade square and back towards the entrance of the Officers' Mess.

Andy continued his pursuit taking in the scene of total chaos around him. His hearing was impaired by the sounds of the air raid sirens and gunfire. He could see several helicopter gunships hovering over the camp firing upon vehicles and troops in the base. There were other helicopters, troop transporters, these touched-down briefly, disgorging assault troops who immediately fanned out and gave covering fire. Seconds later the helicopters headed away keeping low. Andy was sprinting after Crofton just as he heard an unfamiliar whoosh sound; his world went dark.

CHAPTER 21

It started with the sound of a door quietly closing with a gentle click. Next, the smell of a sweet perfume brought his mind to a conscious state. He could feel he was lying in a firm bed. He felt someone adjusting his pillow for a few moments and, after they'd finished, he somehow could tell without opening his eyes they'd moved away. After several seconds, the scent of perfume slowly faded, replaced by the jarring smell of disinfectant and strong bleach. *Where am I? I'm not in the naval base by the Officers Mess? What happened? Where's Crofton? How long have I been here? Where am I?*

Andy slowly opened his eyes. His blurred vision gradually came into focus. He could see from the sparseness of the room, the smell of the strong disinfectant, and sight of the nurse with her back to him in a crisp white uniform and large hat, that he was lying in a hospital bed. Moving only his eyes, Andy looked around the room for further clues. It was small, with only enough space for one bed, the walls were painted a light pastel blue color and the ceiling was painted white.

Andy moved his gaze down. On one wall was a clock with black hour and minute hands and a red second-hand. Andy starred at the clock for several seconds as if trying to figure out a puzzle. Then he realized that the seconds hand wasn't moving. It had either stuck on fifteen, or the clock didn't work. On the main wall, to brighten the otherwise austere setting was a large color print of tall red wildflowers set in a meadow next to a river which fell out of focus into the distance. The only furniture in the room was a gray metal chair pushed into a corner. *Which hospital is this?*

The nurse turned and noticed Andy's eyes were open and spoke to him in Russian, "Good. You're awake. You had us worried for quite some time." Andy tried to speak, but no words came. instead, with a feeling of growing frustration, all he could do was slowly nod. "Can you hear me?" she asked. Andy nodded in reply. "You were involved in an industrial accident. There was an explosion and you were badly hurt. You've been in a coma for three weeks. The good news is you haven't lost any limbs and we believe you'll make a full recovery. You may feel a little confused and anxious. Having those feelings is quite normal. I'm just going to pop out of the room to tell the doctor that you're awake. I'll come back with a glass of water. Drink the water, it will help you talk." She smiled and left Andy alone.

He slowly slid his hands from beneath the sheets and looked at them. He could see recent scaring which had already started to heal. Andy tried to grab the bed sheet to straighten it, but the muscles in his arms ached. Pain radiated from his chest and back. He could feel the onset of a headache. He raised his hands and touched his bandaged head. His attention switched away from himself as the door opened and in walked an elderly man in a sharp dark gray suit. His face etched with concern as he looked down upon him.

With great effort Andy forced himself to speak. "Are you my doctor?" The man laughed for a few seconds. *From that reaction he's not my doctor.*

"Mr. Flint, I'm General Dudek. Do you know who I am?" Andy nodded. "You're in a hospital in Moscow. You've been badly injured and we've had you here for some weeks tending to your injuries. I'm here on behalf of the Russian Government. We are thankful for your resourcefulness in uncovering the plots which my Government was not aware of and bringing them to our attention through Ambassador Rushbrooke. The Russian Government is in your debt." Dudek approached Andy and looked to shake his hand, however, on seeing Andy's injuries he changed his mind and gently patted Andy on the shoulder. "Through your actions we killed and arrested a number of traitors. You prevented a coup and the fall of the Russian Government. I am sorry to say no one outside of a small circle will ever know of how you changed the course of history."

The nurse re-entered the room followed by a tall, thin man wearing a white hospital coat, he had a stethoscope wrapped around his neck and wore a tired expression which went with his unshaven look. The nurse carried a glass of water which she put down at the end of the bed, moved around Dudek to reach Andy and, using both hands under Andy's shoulders, propped him up, then adjusted the metal framed headboard to help support him. She returned to the foot of the bed to collect his water and moving around Dudek she helped Andy sip the cold water. Andy turned to see various drips and tubes to one side which all led towards him. "Thank you," he said quietly. "I'm feeling some pain. Could I have some more pain killers?" The doctor stepped forward and, for him, Dudek stepped out of the way to stand behind the doctor and nurse.

"Mr. Flint. I'm pleased to see you conscious. You've received multiple injuries across your body and you had a serious head injury which meant we had to keep you into an induced coma, just in case, we had to operate to reduce pressure on your brain." Andy smiled as best he could as the doctor continued, "over the next few days, you'll undertake a series of tests to assess the full extent of your injuries, and the results will indicate your long-term prognosis and treatment plan. I don't know whether the nurse told you, but you're very lucky to be alive."

Dudek interjected. "Your government knows you're here, even though we only confirmed your identity last week, they plan to repatriate you once they have the all clear for you to travel from your doctor."

The doctor shook his head and looked deflated as he spoke. "I only hope their care for you is as good as ours." the doctor turned to the nurse, "please increase the dose of his intravenous pain relief from fifty milliliters to seventy-five milliliters per hour." She nodded in response as he continued, "when the additional pain relief makes you comfortable, you'll need to rest. Rest is your friend. I'll come back and see you later." The doctor headed out of the door. The nurse gave Andy a second sip of the water. Andy nodded his appreciation to her. She placed the half full glass at the end of his bed and tended to his drips, making the adjustment the doctor instructed, before making a note of the dosage change on his chart at the end of his bed. With her work done, she looked back at Dudek and then to Andy.

"Please don't talk for long, you do need to rest." After that she headed out of the door leaving Dudek alone again with Andy.

"For quite some time we didn't know who you were. You were wearing unusual camouflage clothes which were torn and burnt and you carried no identification. We initially believed you were one of the military from the naval base. But when we struggled to identify you we looked again at your clothing and determined from your underwear you were probably an American and they found a Glock pistol near you. A few days later the Americans reported you as missing so we put two and two together and figured out who you were."

"How did I end up so badly injured?" Andy asked.

Dudek spread his arms out to the sides and shrugged. "It wasn't us." Dudek pointed to Andy "We didn't do this to you. We had GRU Spetsnaz ground forces deployed by helicopter and they received close air support. But you were injured by something else. Not us."

Andy squinted so he could look closely at Dudek. "What are you saying?"

"An American warship in the Mediterranean Sea fired a single Tomahawk cruise missile. That missile was homing in on your satellite signal and destroyed the Officers' Mess. You were stood next to the building when it struck. You were one of the lucky ones. Somehow the blast didn't kill you." *The strange noise before I was knocked unconscious. A cruise missile? One of ours?* Andy felt confused, the additional drugs slowed his thinking and made him feel light headed as Dudek continued "somebody had that cruise missile programmed with the unique details of your satellite phone and had the authority to command the launch of the missile." *Shit, Langley told Crofton where I was, so Crofton could pick me up? Maybe they wanted to kill Crofton and I was acceptable collateral damage.*

"Did you find another American, called Crofton?" Andy asked.

"No." Dudek shook his head. "There were several bodies which we struggled to identify, but you were the last person we couldn't account for. We didn't capture, or find a body, belonging to anyone called Crofton, or any other Americans for that matter."

"What do you think happened to him?"

"He either got away or if he was injured, someone spirited him away, probably the CIA."

Andy's mind slowly processed what he was being told, the drugs weren't helping. "Why would the CIA do that?"

"Crofton is part of a shadow US Government, have you heard of the Torchbearers?"

Andy racked his thoughts. He knew he'd heard of the name Torchbearers, but his mind was slow... then it struck him. *The conversation in the warehouse between the guards. The Torchbearers were sending the nuclear warheads to Iraq and they sent me to gather the evidence to prove Iraq would have the weapons of mass destruction, but for what reason? Why go to all of this trouble? Could they use it to justify an invasion of Iraq?* "General you didn't answer my question, why would the CIA recover Crofton?"

The Dudek smiled and held a dramatic pause before he revealed more information. "Crofton is still employed by the CIA. He operates in the shadows, a ghost. The Torchbearers run part of the CIA, they have their own programs and no Congressional oversight. Crofton is part of that organization." Dudek remained silent as the realization struck Andy.

It explained why the agency reacted badly when I stepped outside of my brief and stopped the nuclear shells from leaving. They wanted Saddam Hussein to have the nuclear weapons.

Dudek continued, "So, tell me Andy, who can you really trust?"

Andy looked at Dudek's now cold eyes, "I actually don't know the answer to that question."

Dudek's composure changed, "I have some good news for you," Dudek smiled as he reached into his jacket pocket and produced a small rectangular box. "As I said earlier, we are thankful for your services and we are in your debt. To recognize you for your service to the Russian Federation and our Government, President Yeltsin has asked that I present you with our highest award."

"What?" Andy wasn't sure he'd heard Dudek correctly.

Dudek opened the box revealing a gold medal in the shape of a star attached to a white, red and blue ribbon. "Mr. Flint, you are hereby awarded the title 'Hero of the Russian Federation'." Dudek approached Andy, showed him the medal and placed it next to him, then patted him again on the shoulder to avoid shaking his injured hands. Andy was lost for words. "Mr. Flint, you are the first foreigner to receive this award. You are trusted by the Russian Government because you put our Government's survival above your own safety and saved us to fight another day. Since you're a foreigner and can't take up the benefits which a Russian citizen would receive, our President has decreed you can call upon our assistance when you need it and we will do our utmost to respond."

"How do I do that?" Andy asked as the shock slowly wore off.

"Call the Kremlin switchboard and inform them you are a holder of the Hero award. They will ask you who presented it to you. Tell them it was me, General Dudek. They will ask you for a code. The answer is October 1917."

"Got it." Andy replied.

"Do not share what I've told you with anyone."

"I won't."

"Only call if it's a life and death situation and we're your last throw of the dice. Don't call because you've missed your last train home and need a ride!"

"I understand. Please thank your President."

Dudek laughed, "I don't believe he'll remember. He'd been drinking heavily when he decided to give you the award." The door opened and a man in a dark blue suit, white shirt and red tie entered the room. His short, neatly trimmed hair and his muscular physique indicated to Andy this was one of Dudek's men. The man whispered quietly into the General's ear and left the room. "You have a visitor, so I have to leave, but before I go, it would be remiss if I do not offer you the opportunity to work for us. I can tell you that, if you do, your career in the CIA would continue to advance and, you would be able to provide us with valuable information. I can make it worth your while." Dudek raised his right hand and repeatedly rubbed his thumb over the top of his middle and forefingers, indicating money. "A few hundred thousand dollars here and there, also we can call in all sorts of favors to make your life better, without the need for you to pay a cent.

You'd be surprised at how well connected we are. All I ask is for you to think about it."

I'm honored to be so highly thought of. But I ain't no traitor to my country. "Thank you General, but I can't accept your offer."

"I understand, you're a patriot. Regardless of that, once again I must thank you, on behalf of the Russian Government, for your actions." Dudek quietly slipped out of the room. Andy felt the fatigue, as through someone had removed a plug and all his energy had drained out. Then Ambassador Rushbrooke walked into the room with Carrie Roper following closely behind. He looked at them through heavy eyelids, the Ambassador spoke first.

"I'm glad we found you, we thought you'd vanished off the face of the earth, the doctor says you'll recover." Andy nodded as the Ambassador continued, "So, to cheer you up, and give you some much needed sugar, I've brought you these," he held up a candy box. "You did your country a great service at that naval base. Your actions saved countless lives and helped crush an attempted coup. Our President is grateful and is talking about issuing some honors. You could see something good out of this." Rushbrooke's eyes wandered down to the Russian medal. "I see the Russian's got there first." Andy nodded as his eyes got heavier.

Roper cut in, "However, there are some at Langley who think you disobeyed orders and went rogue again. So not everyone sees you as a hero. If you come back, I can't guarantee they'll put you in the field or, if they do, that you'll be with the Russian desk."

Rushbrooke tried to lighten the mood, "We're arranging to have you flown home … Andy!" But Andy had fallen into a deep sleep.

CHAPTER 22

Andy's room was in a private hospital in Washington DC and had more color, furniture and a large television with cable when compared to his room in Moscow. His doctors were confident he'd make a full recovery, but it would take time. They'd started physiotherapy sessions to help get him moving again. Counseling sessions had begun and would finish when the psych team were satisfied that he had come to terms with the mental trauma associated with losing his girlfriend and co-workers, together with his two near death experiences in a such a short timescale.

The one thing he found unusual was they'd given him the name, *John Doe*, for some unexplained reason. When the CIA arrived to repatriate him, they told him it was for *'operational reasons'* and they'd tell him when he could use his name again. This nagged at him but he hadn't told the psych team, preferring to keep this to himself. His thoughts were interrupted by the door opening and his regular nurse, Jenny Carlton, entering. She had been his primary care giver since he'd arrived at the facility.

She checked the chart at the end of his bed, then came to his side and, using his bedside thermometer, checked his temperature. While the thermometer recorded his temperature from under his tongue, she held his left wrist and took his pulse using her other hand to count the seconds on her watch. She noted the result on his chart before removing the thermometer, turning it slightly to clearly see its reading. "Hmm, still a bit high, but your temperature is lower than earlier which is good." She wrote the reading on his chart, then returned the thermometer to its bedside holder. "I've got to get your next dose of medication. Do you need any pain relief?"

"No, I'm good. Um ... I never thanked you for that Dictaphone you got me. I just wanted a way to record my thoughts," he lied, "thoughts and memories just pop in and out of my head and I can't remember them again. The Dictaphone helps me remember when I play them back. It's helpful when I'm talking to the psych team."

"John that's fine. If there's anything else you'd like help with, just let me know." She gave his hand a gentle squeeze. "Let me go and get your medicines." She left the room for a few minutes and returned carrying a small plastic cup containing several pills of different sizes and color along with a glass of water. Andy's hands had healed enough to allow him to hold the glass as the nurse handed him the cup. He could see she was watching him carefully to make sure he was taking all his medications. When he'd finished the last of his pills, she noted the time against each medication on his chart and returned it to the end of his bed. "I'll be back later, if you need anything, press the buzzer and one of us will come along to check in with you." Andy knew the other nurses, but he got along better with Carlton, she was more his age and he liked her.

Carlton approached the door to leave but as she did so it opened, startling her and causing her to take a step back. An older man in a gray suit and receding gray hair held the door open indicating she should leave. He reeked 'Agency' and, as he watched Nurse Carlton leave, Andy secretly switched on the Dictaphone and placed it out of view under his top bed sheet. The gray man closed the door behind him and turned to face Andy. "Hello Andrew. I'm Don James from the Department of Strategic Outcomes. We are part of the agency but you've probably never heard of us."

"No I haven't."

"See we've been doing our jobs: No one should know we exist."

James laughed. Andy smiled politely. "The Department of Strategic Outcomes was formed in the fifties at the height of the cold war under Allen Dulles, when Mc Carthey was doing his thing. We are still here today, doing important work for our country and because of the importance of what we do we are kept well away from any scrutiny." James smiled at Andy and continued. "What is unusual, for our clandestine agency, is that we have both public and private sponsors, which means we have access to resources other agencies can only dream of, and that means we have very deep pockets. You know what?"

"No." Andy realized he'd replied to a rhetorical question. *Not smart!*

"We're always on the lookout for fresh talent to join us and you've come onto our radar. Very few people get approached by us, Andy, so take it as a massive compliment that I'm here to recruit you. The Russians thought you were dead after they murdered Tex Striker. The US Government thought you were dead for nearly three weeks when you were in the Ukraine and then Moscow and, your here as a John Doe. You've been marked as dead more times than a cat with nine lives." James laughed. *Where's this going?* Andy thought. "I'm going to present you with a life changing opportunity. All you have to do is listen to what I have to say … and then make a choice."

"Okay … I'm listening." Andy replied cautiously.

"The Department of Strategic Outcomes is an off-the-books part of the CIA and part of a wider secret program. Our purpose is to find ways to ensure our military, security and defense industries are relevant and ready to respond in today's uncertain world. They call us the Torchbearers as we fearlessly beat a trail forwards through the darkness to keep America strong. We hold the beacon of light to ward off danger so that the American people can safely go about their daily lives." *Apart from Crofton, my first contact with a Torchbearer.* "I'd like you to make a life changing choice: join us and be a Torchbearer for democracy, protecting the American way of life." Jones paused to let his words hang between them before continuing, "but with that choice, there is a sacrifice you have to make. You have to leave your past behind. You have to assume a new identity and never look back. The alternative is to resume your life as Andrew Flint and go back to your previous role at the CIA. You will never see or hear from us again and, since we don't exist, you will never be able to find us. You have a decision to make but this is a one time, once in a lifetime offer."

"The man who murdered my colleagues in Luhansk and my girlfriend; the same man who was in league with the rogue Russian military, John Crofton, he told me he was a Torchbearer."
James's confident composure flickered momentarily with uncertainty before returning. "Sometimes it's the bigger picture which is important and, unfortunately, there is unavoidable collateral damage. Yes, Crofton is a Torchbearer, but the sacrifices those people made, will help keep our nation strong. Their sacrifices will help keep our nation safe. I'm sorry they paid for it with their lives, but it was necessary." Andy felt he was being pressured into a decision. If he joined them, he could learn about them, and maybe take them down from within; or, he could simply go back to the job he enjoyed and forget about them. "What do you say?"

***

Jack Masters, FBI Director of Counter Espionage, arrived at his office as usual at seven thirty, beating the worst of the morning downtown traffic. He collected his post, which the overnight staff had sorted for him. One item caught his attention, a plain white envelope with his name written on it in blue ink. There were no other identifying markings on the envelope. He felt the envelope and believed it to contain a small rectangular object. With his curiosity piqued, in the privacy of his office he tore the envelope open causing a small plastic cassette to fall onto his table along with a business card. Masters looked at the card and saw it was from Andy Flint. He had the title NGO Coordinator with the Office of Overseas Development. Masters picked up the Dictaphone cassette and held it up to the light. "What have we here?"

***

At a discreet private hospital in Geneva, Switzerland, a nurse carefully unwrapped the bandages from the head of a patient following cosmetic surgery. As she finished she stepped back to give their patient more space. "Mr. Crofton, the surgery went well, you're looking very good."

***

Excerpt from The Makarov File.

PROLOGUE

The sound of their footsteps echoed off the drab grey concrete walls of the decaying nineteen sixties buildings which closed in and surrounded them. The dull, iridescent glow of the street lights pooled on the ground, guiding their route through the sleeping city. Snow clearing teams had been busy with unusually heavy snowfalls, though the remaining ice on the sidewalk made Amanda tread carefully to avoid slipping.

The cold air cleared her head from the effects of the jet lag following her flight from Washington that afternoon. She wasn't as well prepared for the cold as her companion and despite her thick woollen hat, the cold slowly seeped through her clothing. She regretted leaving the warmth of her hotel room, but as the senior analyst on the Russian desk in Langley, she had to be here.

They were to identify the head of a fast-growing mafia organisation originating in St Petersburg. Amanda's sources had finally given her a solid lead and she had jumped to confirm the location of the organisation's headquarters. Her companion, the Head of the CIA station in Moscow, had ignored her request to follow her lead on her own and had decided to accompany her. Only after he threatened to deny her access to the operation had she relented and allowed Bruce Chester to come along.

The lead pointed to an industrial zone eight miles east of the city centre. They were to scout the area on foot before returning with more agents should the lead prove fruitful. With three blocks still to cover, Amanda noticed two men struggling under the weight of a large roll of carpet a little way in front of their path. As they got closer, Amanda could see the two were moving the carpet from a unit next to the sidewalk into the rear of a large flat back delivery truck.

The shapes of the two men became clearer, the noises of their effort grew louder as the agents approached. The carpet took up most of the sidewalk, forcing the pair towards the unit, into the shadows of the building. Bruce pressed close to her and then fell behind, allowing her to walk in front of him to pass the carpet and the laborers. She glanced at one of the men who'd been attempting to move the carpet and caught their eye.

They'd stopped moving the carpet.

Out from the shadows, six well-built men wearing ski masks moved in on them.

Amanda felt a cloth go over her mouth and nose. She smelled the sweet chemical scent of chloroform. She struggled and tried to rip it away, noticing Bruce doing the same, but the vice like grip of her attacker was too strong. She grabbed at the man, clawing at his clothing. Her hands got heavier and heavier, the fight slowly draining from her as she breathed in the fumes. Her eyelids became too heavy to keep open and she fell into a deep, peaceful sleep.

***

The police had been drawn to the Blue Bridge by an early morning jogger who saw what appeared to be a body floating in the freezing shallows of the Moyka River.

It had been confirmed quickly after they'd arrived at the scene that the strange shape floating in the river was that of a man dressed in thick winter clothing. According to the Forensics experts, summoned to the scene before their first coffee, he'd been in the river for a few days. As little remained of his face, the ID in his wallet provided the only clue to his identity when they emptied the pockets of the corpse at the start of the post-mortem. It identified the body as that of Bruce Chester.

The Senior Lieutenant assigned to the case watched with a stony indifference as they cut open the cadaver on the table in front of him. A Private who'd entered half way through the process, needed to recover from the sight of the bloated corpse being examined. "The ID is real. He worked for the US Trade and Investment Council."

The Lieutenant had surmised as much after a quick examination of the ID after it had been found. "Has the US Consulate been informed?"

"The Captain's calling them now." The Private paused, eyes drifting back to the grisly spectacle of the autopsy. "The Consulate will contact his next of kin."

The senior officer nodded "We'll have an American coming to investigate the murder soon enough." His tone held a note of displeasure. "If only it were a robbery."

"You don't think it was a robbery which had gone wrong Sir?"

The Lieutenant gave him an incredulous look. "They tortured him. He still had his wallet." He shook his head "Someone wanted us to find him. Someone wants to send a message to the Americans and they're using us to deliver it."

The Lieutenant blew into his hands to warm them from the chill of the mortuary. "They'll send more Americans here to investigate."

He turned to the Private, looked him over from his pale face down to his shiny new boots before turning to leave the room. As he left, he spoke over his shoulder, his voice weary "We're going to be busy."

***

If you enjoyed reading Double Cross, I'd really appreciate you leaving an honest review. Reviews help other readers make their decisions on whether the book they are about to read would be right for them. Reviews also help authors improve their visibility within on-line bookstores and your review will help grow my writing career. Success will help me write more and be spurred on to be quicker, which means more of my great stories for you to read.

To leave your review, please go to:

https://www.amazon.com/review/create-review?asin=**123455**

If you'd like to sign up to my newsletter, then please click on the link below and enter your email details. I'll respect your privacy and not share your details with others and you can unsubscribe at any time by emailing me and placing *'Unsubscribe'* in the subject field.

https://www.subscribepage.com/peter-kozmar.com

Alternatively you can also follow me on social media @peter.kozmar or for those using LinkedIn, look out for Peter Kozmar.

***

About the Author

Peter was born near Manchester in the North West of England into a working class family. He studied Engineering at University where he joined the British Army.

During his service he worked in Russia, Ukraine, South Africa and a number of other colourful locations. After reaching the rank of Major, he resigned his Commission and moved with his family to New Zealand where he led an active, outdoors life. However, a skiing accident meant he had time on his hands and started writing.

Peter lives in Wellington, New Zealand. His kids have now left home leaving him with his wife and two mischievous Labrador's, Brecon and Pembroke.

Made in the USA
Las Vegas, NV
12 January 2023

65511982R00097